"How do you get used to it?" Jason asked her.

"The darkness," he explained when he realized that Addie had tilted her head in his direction and was giving him a quizzical look.

"Oh, it's not always so dark," Addie assured the builder.

"Yeah, in the daytime there's the sun," he deadpanned.

Addie looked at him patiently. "I wasn't talking about that. Some of the time," she went on, "there's a full moon out and that casts a lot of light."

"But most of the time there isn't a full moon," he reminded her. "Like when there's a new moon out and the area is pitch-black."

Addie really didn't see anything wrong with that. "Oh, I don't know. That can be pretty romantic at times," she pointed out. "Haven't you ever been out with a woman and wished that the surrounding area wasn't quite as brightly lit as it was?" she asked as she turned toward him. "In a way, the darkness makes people bolder. It gives them permission to do things that they might not be brave enough to attempt to do in the light of day," Addie maintained.

And then he moved closer toward her. As if on cue, her heart began pounding. Jason slowly reached out to frame her face. Addie anticipated what was going to happen next.

She stood very, very still.

What happened next happened almost in slow motion.

Jason bent over her and then his lips covered hers. Addie's breath caught in her throat, his went on pounding.

Wildly.

D0188987

Dear Reader,

Welcome back to the little town of Forever. The good news is that the hardworking, friendly citizens are finally getting a general hospital of their own. That means they will no longer have to travel over fifty miles when time is of the essence in life-and-death cases.

Of course, along with the erection of this all-important new edifice, there is also the all-important romance. Ellie and Neil's (from *Secrets of Forever*) wedding has been put on hold until Miss Joan is strong enough to take over the wedding arrangements. And there are two new romances, too! After years of suffering from guilt, Miss Joan's younger sister, Zelda, finally falls for a good man, the widower Eduardo Montenegro. Contrasting this couple's slow progress toward love is Adelyn Montenegro, Ellie's sister, and Jason Eastwood, Neil's cousin who has been tapped to be Neil's best man. Their path is more tempestuous. So there are actually three weddings in this book, as well as a new, much-needed hospital. How's that for a happily-ever-after?

As always, I thank you for picking up one of my books. I hope you find reading it as enjoyable as I found writing it. And from the bottom of my heart, I wish you someone to love who loves you back.

Love,

Marie

The Best Man
in Texas

—

MARIE FERRARELLA

HARLEQUIN
SPECIAL
EDITION

Recycling programs for this product may not exist in your area.

ISBN-13: 978-1-335-40819-8

The Best Man in Texas

Copyright © 2021 by Marie Rydzynski-Ferrarella

This edition published by arrangement with Harlequin Books S.A.

For questions and comments about the quality of this book, please contact us at CustomerService@Harlequin.com.

Harlequin Enterprises ULC
22 Adelaide St. West, 40th Floor
Toronto, Ontario M5H 4E3, Canada
www.Harlequin.com

Printed in U.S.A.

USA TODAY bestselling and RITA® Award–winning author **Marie Ferrarella** has written more than three hundred books for Harlequin, some under the name Marie Nicole. Her romances are beloved by fans worldwide. Visit her website, marieferrarella.com.

Books by Marie Ferrarella

Harlequin Special Edition

Forever, Texas

The Cowboy's Lesson in Love
The Lawman's Romance Lesson
Her Right Hand Cowboy
Secrets of Forever

Matchmaking Mamas

Coming Home for Christmas
Dr. Forget-Me-Not
Twice a Hero, Always Her Man
Meant to Be Mine
A Second Chance for the Single Dad
Christmastime Courtship
Engagement for Two
Adding Up to Family
Bridesmaid for Hire
Coming to a Crossroads
The Late Bloomer's Road to Love

Visit the Author Profile page
at Harlequin.com for more titles.

To

The Real Ellie and Addie

Two Adorable Little Girls

Who Won My Heart

From The Day They Were

Each Born

Never Lose That Special Magic

That Is You

Love,

G-Mama

Prologue

It was all coming together.

Thinking about it, Dr. Neil Eastwood smiled to himself. After what had seemed like an endless wait, Neil could finally—*finally*—see the goalpost. His wedding to Ellie was no longer a nebulous mirage shimmering seductively off in the distance. It would actually be here in thirty days.

If he was being honest with himself, he would have preferred that the wedding would be here within a day or two. But in the last six months, he had learned that things didn't exactly move all that fast in Forever, Texas.

Not unless it was an emergency that involved Miss Joan, the town's undisputed matriarch. And although this did involve Miss Joan, it wasn't her opinion but her health that had been the problem these last six months.

To make things more complicated, he was the one who had to sign off on her, the one who had been brought in to operate on the woman in order to stabilize her heart and now had the last word when it came to her ability to get back to life as she knew it.

Who would have ever imagined, Neil now thought, that his own heart would come into play when he had gotten involved in what had amounted to this selfless act—he hadn't charged Miss Joan for the operation.

But his heart had definitely gotten involved. He had fallen in love with Elliana Montenegro, the feisty, independent pilot who had flown out to fetch him so he could attend to the opinionated matriarch.

He had quickly learned that Miss Joan all but ran Forever.

And now the woman was putting together their wedding in her own inimitable way. Quite honestly, he could have sworn that planning this wedding had actually contributed to and insured her complete recovery. It didn't take him very long to look beneath the layers and see that the crusty Miss Joan really enjoyed leaving her mark on people's lives.

The added bonus to having saved a life was that if it hadn't been for his coming out to attend to Miss Joan, he would have never met the woman of his dreams. He certainly wouldn't be anxiously waiting now to finalize their union.

The smile on Neil's lips intensified. All that was left to do on his end was to secure his best man.

He knew just the man for the job, had known him ever since they had been young boys together, growing up in New York City.

It occurred to Neil as he put his cousin's number into his cell phone that he hadn't talked to Jason in over six months.

Had that much time really gone by? Neil caught himself wondering. It seemed like one day he was answering an old friend's request and getting on a plane to Texas, the next he was getting involved with a bright-eyed, sexy pilot, and suddenly, the entire structure of his life had completely refocused.

Hearing the phone on the other end being answered, Neil straightened in his office chair.

"Jason?" he asked the moment he heard his cousin say "Hello?"

There was a pause on the other end and then a deep, puzzled male voice asked, "Neil?"

"Yeah, it's me," Neil confirmed happily, leaning back in the chair again.

"Wow," Jason marveled, happy to hear from his cousin. "It's really you. I was beginning to think you had fallen into an abyss. So what's it been, nine months?"

"Six," Neil corrected.

Jason laughed softly under his breath. "Six," he repeated, then confessed, "I've been busy myself. I guess I kind of lost track of time. Where are you these days?"

There was a time when their paths crossed with a fair amount of regularity, but that hadn't been for a while now.

"I'm still in Forever, Texas," Neil replied, just about to launch into his request. This, he was certain, was bound to knock Jason's socks clean off.

"Sorry to hear that," Jason said, cutting in. "The locals decide they couldn't pass up the chance of having a cardiac surgeon in their midst and took you prisoner?"

"Not exactly, although technically I am a prisoner—" Neil began, only to have his cousin cut him off again.

Jason wasn't sure if his cousin was putting him on or not. "You're kidding, right?" he asked Neil.

Rather than explain his comment, Neil went right to the heart of the reason behind his call. "Listen, Jason, what are you doing in a month?"

The question stopped Jason in his tracks. He assumed that his cousin was asking him about his work. While the rest of the family had gone into some discipline of medicine, including his parents, Jason had gone into the practical aspect of building and outfitting the medical facilities where surgeries could take place. Lately he had been building or updating hospitals

"As it is," Jason told his cousin, "I'm just wrapping up my latest project in Staten Island and looking for something new to work on. Why? What's up?"

Neil felt that although there was no one to witness it at the moment, his grin would split his face. "I want you to fly out here and be my best man."

Neil heard the sound of the cell phone being dropped, then the sound of that same phone being grabbed and picked up again.

"Jason? Are you still there?" Neil asked. He

had figured that his cousin would be surprised, but not *this* surprised.

"Yeah, yeah, I'm still here. I thought I heard you saying something about wanting me to be your best man," Jason explained, certain he must have misheard. He had just assumed that he and his cousin were eternal bachelors.

"I did and I do. Will you?" Neil asked.

When he spoke, Jason sounded nothing less than stunned. "This must have been some rescue mission you were on," he said, referring to his cousin's last communication via email.

Neil laughed. "You don't know the half of it. But I'm more than willing to fill you in on all the details once you get here. Which leads me back to my first question—can you come?"

"To your wedding?" Jason asked incredulously, finally getting his bearings back. "Just try and stop me. All I need to know is exactly where and when," he said, remembering the boyhood pact they had made long ago to be there if the other ever found "someone dumb enough to marry you." They had been ten and twelve at the time.

Neil quickly gave his cousin the date and the location, and added, "Oh, and Ellie and I will meet you at the airport so she can fly you in the rest of the way."

"Fly me in the rest of the way?" Jason repeated. "Why?"

"There's no connecting flight to Forever," Neil explained. "The closest airport is over fifty miles away."

That caught Jason off guard. He had been aware, from what Jason had said before he left, that Forever was a small town. But he had just assumed the airport was only a hop, skip and jump away from the place.

"You're kidding, right?" Jason asked.

"No." Neil thought his cousin was referring to his bride-to-be doing the piloting. "Ellie has her own plane. Like I said, I'll explain everything when you get here," he promised again. And then he thought about the town needing a hospital. "And, if you're interested, I've also got a really great project for you to sink your teeth into."

This whole proposition was beginning to sound more and more enticing, Jason thought, as he looked at the calendar on his desk.

"I can be there in three weeks," he told Neil, his mind already making all the necessary arrangements. It wouldn't hurt to come out early so that he and Neil could spend some time catching up before everything took off. "Oh, and Neil?"

"Yes?" Neil asked, preparing to terminate his call.

"I'm really happy for you," Jason said warmly, even though he was still trying to get used to the idea that Neil was actually getting married.

Neil laughed, picturing what life would be like four weeks in the future. The thought definitely excited him.

"Yeah," he answered, "me, too."

Chapter One

"So you're telling me that Neil's younger cousin is planning on coming out to Forever a week early?" Ellie's younger sister, Adelyn, asked her in surprise.

This was the first she was hearing about this, Addie thought. But then, she had been extremely busy these last few months. Aside from helping to get ready for Ellie's wedding, she had finally completed her business degree in what had been lightning speed. In the last six months, Addie had done what amounted to a total about-face. But then, once she decided to do something, there was just no deterring her from her path.

And Addie had witnessed so many changes taking place in Ellie's own life. It was finding out that Ellie was getting married that finally convinced her to go after her own degree. She felt the need to take charge of her own life.

And, just like that, getting that degree was suddenly what really seemed to matter to her.

Her priorities were shifting.

Addie's mouth curved suddenly. Who would have thought? she mused.

Meanwhile, Ellie kept her face averted as she continued cleaning her plane. Knowing nothing about him except that he was very important to Neil, she wanted to create a good first impression on Neil's cousin.

As she worked, she answered her sister's question.

"That's the word—early," Ellie replied. "Neil hasn't seen his cousin in almost seven months. They were always very close when they were kids. According to Neil, they occasionally lost track of each other here and there, but they always managed to get together whenever they could," Ellie told her sister. "Actually, they seem closer than brothers," she said.

"The wedding gives them both the perfect excuse, especially since Jason told Neil he just finished work on a project." Ellie smiled, thinking how excited Neil had been, telling her about the plan he had come up with. "That was when Neil asked him to be his best man. Coming out a week early is the perfect opportunity for the two of them to catch up on each other's lives before the big day takes place."

Her curiosity aroused, Addie asked her sister, "Is his cousin a doctor, too?"

Ellie shook her head. "The rest of his cousin's family are all in the medical profession. Jason is the 'black sheep.' He focuses on working on buildings."

"Buildings," Addie repeated. "You mean like he gets businesses up and running?" she asked, trying to understand what Neil's cousin actually did for a living.

"No," Ellie answered. "He switched his major and got, among other things, a degree in structural engineering. Lately, he's been overseeing building or renovating hospitals."

Addie started thinking about all the conversations she had overheard about Forever needing to have its own hospital. This was beginning to sound better and better. "He builds hospitals?" Addie asked, making sure she wasn't just reading into this.

Ellie put down her cloth. "That's what Neil said. I didn't get too much of a chance to talk to him about his cousin."

"Why not?" Addie asked. She would have thought that would be the main topic, given that the wedding was almost here and, according to Ellie, Neil's cousin was going to be here even sooner.

"Frankly, Neil was too busy reviewing Marion McCarthy's recent records on her heart," Ellie told her. "The woman has been having chest pains." Ellie laughed softly to herself as she shook her head. "It seems now that we have a cardiologist in our midst, everyone who is experiencing chest pains is coming in for EKGs and EEGs to make sure they're not going to keel over."

Ellie looked up to see her sister rolling her eyes at her comment. "What?" she asked, looking at Addie curiously.

Her sister frowned slightly. "You and Neil are still in the romantic stage of your lives together, Ellie," she pointed out. "And I'm really thrilled that you two found each other. Just don't let Neil's cousin—or anyone else, for that matter—divert your attention from each other. At least wait until you've had a chance to spend your first year together. You'll have the rest of your lives to deal with other people's interference," she predicted.

Ellie didn't look convinced. Neil was a doctor and she was very proud of him. In her opinion, trying to get him to focus on her just didn't seem right. "That would be selfish."

There were times, Addie thought, that Ellie came off like a saint, although she would never say as much to her sister.

"No," Addie contradicted, looking into her sister's eyes. "That would be wonderful. You deserve it, Ellie."

Ellie couldn't help but laugh. "Okay, who are you and what have you done with my sister?"

Addie raised her shoulders, then let them drop. "Well, you're always telling me to grow up. So I just decided to finally take you up on your advice."

"Next time, don't do it so fast or I'm liable to get whiplash," Ellie warned. Picking up the cleaning rag she had been using, she turned her attention back to putting the finishing touches on the plane.

By all accounts, the plane looked spick-and-span. But this was her first time meeting Neil's cousin and she wanted to create a good first impression, especially since the man seemed to mean so much to Neil.

"By the way, are you still working on what you plan to do with your degree?" Ellie asked. At last count, there were still an endless number of career paths for her sister to choose from.

Addie nodded. "Yes, I am."

Ellie knew what that meant. "In other words, you're still debating," she concluded.

"Let's just say I'm keeping my options open," Addie answered. She had always been very handy when it came to building things, as well as having a knack for getting things done. She was attempting to figure out how to marry those things with her business degree.

Ellie merely smiled. "Good idea," she responded to her sister's options-open comment. Despite everything, things hadn't changed all that much. Addie still had no desire to close the door firmly shut on anything. That was part of the reason that Addie didn't make any hard-and-fast decisions.

Well, at least her sister had finally gotten her degree. That hadn't changed. Once Addie made up her mind, she had put her studies on the fast track, picking up courses she had dropped earlier and making short work of them. It was almost as if she had totally given up sleeping.

At times, it felt to Ellie as if her sister had gone from party girl to quick study with very few steps in between.

"So when are we picking up Neil's cousin?"

Addie asked. Taking a rag in her hand, she joined her sister's cleaning effort.

"'We?'" Ellie asked, surprised by the question. "You're coming with us?"

"Of course, I'm coming with you," Addie answered, wondering why Ellie could even ask that question. "This guy's going to be part of the family. I think I should meet the man sooner than later," Addie pointed out. Besides, she couldn't help wondering if the man was as good-looking as Neil was.

It amazed Ellie how much Addie had changed in the last six months. It was almost as if her upcoming marriage had made her sister alter the way she viewed absolutely everything.

Just then, their grandfather, Eduardo Montenegro, declared in a booming voice, "The wedding is almost here," as he walked into the barn that he and Addie had converted into a hangar for Ellie's secondhand plane.

Eduardo stopped between his granddaughters, then pressed a kiss to each one of their temples. "I cannot believe that the time went by so quickly," the older man said with a sentimental smile.

Except for an occasional helping hand from Miss Joan, the man had single-handedly raised the girls since their parents had died in a car accident. Ellie had been six at the time, while Addie had been four.

Proud of them both, Eduardo felt a tug on his heart as he slipped an arm around each granddaughter's shoulder. "Your grandmother would have loved to have been here to see this," he told them with feeling. "She loved both of you so very much."

At the mention of her grandmother, Ellie looked a little misty. The girls' grandmother had been in the vehicle with her parents when they had been killed by a trucker, who had lost control of his truck.

And Eduardo hadn't even had any time to grieve properly. There had been two little granddaughters to raise and take care of. Ellie and Addie and his ranch had taken up all of his time, and it had been a good thing. It allowed Eduardo to sublimate his pain until he was finally able to deal with it.

"I can't even remember what she looked like," Addie lamented in a rare moment of sadness.

Her grandfather looked at her in surprise. He'd forgotten how young Addie had been at the time.

"Just look in the mirror," he told Addie. "You will be able to see your grandmother. You look just like she did when she was your age."

Ellie didn't want her grandfather to dwell on the

bittersweet feelings that memories of her grandmother always created within him. So she changed the subject.

"Are you coming with us to the airport to pick up Neil's cousin?" Ellie asked him. Before he could answer, she added cheerfully, "Addie's going to be coming with us."

"No, I will let you kids go without me. I am going to stay home and prepare a special lunch for all of you," he volunteered.

"No need for you to work hard like that, Grandpa. Why don't we just pick up something at Miss Joan's?" Ellie suggested.

"As a matter of fact, when I mentioned to Zelda that I wanted to prepare lunch for all of you, she insisted on coming over and doing that for me. Tomorrow is her day off," Eduardo added quickly to keep his granddaughters from asking more questions.

Ellie smiled as she exchanged looks with her sister.

"Sounds like a good idea," Ellie agreed, glancing toward Addie for confirmation.

Addie wasn't altogether sure if she was picking up the right messages when it came to Miss Joan's sister. One moment it felt as if her grandfather was actually beginning to fall for the woman. The next moment Addie was convinced that she was just imagining all this in her head.

One step at a time, Addie counseled herself. Right now, if she was being honest, everything felt as if it was moving much too fast. She had a feeling that she was allowing her mind to run away with her, creating scenarios that had no business being here.

This was all going to settle down when the wedding was finally over and behind them, she promised herself.

Besides, Addie thought, Neil had plans to get this proposed hospital off the ground and she had a really good feeling that would finally happen when Neil put his cousin in charge.

This was all going to be a huge step for Forever. Things really seemed to be moving quickly, she couldn't help thinking. It wasn't all that many years ago that in order to get medical treatment for any reason, the town residents would have to travel fifty miles to get to a clinic or hospital.

Ellie finished preparing her plane and put away the rags she was using. "Are you going to need any help, Grandpa?" Ellie asked.

Her grandfather smiled at Ellie's offer. "All you need to do is make sure you have your plane all gassed up and ready to go tomorrow so you can all fly out and meet your fiancé's best man," Eduardo reminded his older granddaughter.

Guilt pricked at Addie's conscience. "I could stay and cook," she offered, although there was a lack of enthusiasm in her voice. She really meant well, but at the same time, Addie was aware that she really didn't have a talent for cooking.

Her grandfather was equally aware of that. "Do not take offense, sweetheart, but we do not want to chase away Neil's cousin. You are good at a great many things. Unfortunately, cooking is not one of them."

Addie sighed. "I would take offense, Grandpa, if it wasn't so true," she confessed. She flashed the man a smile. "Just make sure that Miss Zelda doesn't wind up working you into the ground."

"I will be lucky if that lady allows me to get anywhere near the food," Eduardo confided. "Once I put the horses away, Miss Joan's sister and I are going to go shopping. From what I have learned, the woman really enjoys preparing food. She even took over for Miss Joan while Miss Joan was getting well," he reminded the girls.

"We know, Grandpa. She was a real help, although I think Miss Joan was a little put off by the fact that her sister was able to pitch in so readily,"

Addie said. "Nobody likes to think that they can be easily replaced."

"Miss Joan is not so small-minded," Eduardo protested.

"Not exactly so small-minded," Ellie explained. When her grandfather looked at her quizzically, Ellie decided to remind him of the past event that had gone down between the two sisters. "You forget everything that occurred between them. Zelda ran off with Miss Joan's husband and their son. Not that Miss Joan's husband was remotely a decent man," Ellie concluded.

"But all that happened so long ago in the past," Eduardo said to his granddaughters. "And Miss Joan is married now. There comes a time when people need to just forgive and forget things that happened to them in the past."

"Miss Joan is trying," Addie told her grandfather, giving the woman her due. "But sometimes, no matter how hard people try to forget them, old wounds surface." She smiled at the man who had been part of their lives forever. "You forget, Grandpa. Not everyone is as forgiving as you."

Eduardo refused to allow his granddaughters' words to change his mind. He believed in the basic goodness of people.

"All they need to do is just look into their hearts," he told them.

Moved, Ellie threw her arms around her grandfather and hugged him. "You're one in a million, Grandpa. If anyone ever tries to hurt you, they'll have me to reckon with."

"They'll have *both* of us to reckon with," Addie pointedly corrected.

Eduardo's face grew sunnier as he looked from one granddaughter to the other. "I will be sure to warn them," he said to the girls. "Now, if you will excuse me, I really do have things to do," he explained. "You know how I do not like to leave things until the last minute."

"We know, Grandpa," Ellie dutifully replied. "We were the only girls in school who had to do homework as soon as we came home, even before you had us doing our chores."

"I do not think that that hurt either of you," Eduardo told his granddaughters. He knew that Ellie believed that, but he wasn't so sure about Addie. Yes, she had changed, but he didn't know just how much she had changed.

"At the time, I wasn't all that sure that it didn't," Addie said quite honestly.

"But I am sure that you are now," Eduardo

cheerfully shot over his shoulder as he left the hangar.

Addie continued to watch the man walk away. She bit her lower lip. "Maybe I should go with Grandpa to the store," she mused.

Ellie spun around to face her sister. "Don't you dare," she warned. "Grandpa's a fully grown man and he'll be just fine. He doesn't need you to run interference for him."

Addie wasn't all that sure that was the case. "But he might—"

"No, no *but*," Ellie sternly told her sister. "Just remember, that man never rode roughshod over you, so don't you dare ride roughshod over him," she warned her sister. Pinning her with a look meant to keep Addie in her place, she said, "You know I'm right. And just to make sure, you're coming with Neil and me tomorrow."

"You're really not worried about Grandpa and Zelda?" Addie asked.

"No, I'm worried about the damage you could do if you get carried away. Look at it this way— this is like watching him take baby steps. Grandpa needs this more than you need to keep him tied to your side." She gave Addie a look. "Do I make myself clear?" she asked.

Addie sighed. She knew that Ellie was making

sense. They owed everything to that man, and in their own way, they each wanted to protect him and keep their grandfather from being hurt. In all this time, they had never even remotely seen the man "keeping company" with any woman, much less flirting with the possibility of getting serious with any of them.

"All right, you win," Addie murmured.

Ellie grinned at her sister. "Glad to hear that," she declared as she and Addie walked out of the hangar, arm in arm.

Chapter Two

Addie stood next to Neil and her sister, scanning the airport for what felt like the tenth or eleventh time. She was looking for the very handsome man in the photograph that Neil had shown her. It looked as if the nonstop flight coming in from JFK in New York had completely emptied out and there was still no sign of Neil's cousin.

"Do you think that your cousin missed his flight?" Addie asked. That seemed to be the only reason she could think of as to why the man hadn't come walking down the ramp out of the airplane yet.

Neil frowned. It was obvious that he was concerned about his cousin as well, but for now, he wasn't about to dwell on what might have gone wrong.

"Addie," the cardiologist pointed out kindly, "there are a dozen different ways for people to communicate these days. I'm sure that if Jason had missed his flight for some reason, he would have gotten in touch with me by now," Neil assured the two women, looking from Addie to his fiancée.

Addie glanced in her sister's direction. She saw Ellie shaking her head and she knew that her sister was telling her to back off. Addie did…in part.

"Still, something might have come up," Addie pointed out.

"Well, unless the power grid went down…" Neil began, only to have Addie tug on his sleeve. He stopped talking and asked her, "What?"

"Is that him?" Addie asked. She indicated a confident, tall, impossibly good-looking, dark blond-haired man wearing a light gray suit. The man was walking down a near-empty airplane ramp.

Neil turned in the direction that Addie had indicated, fully prepared to deny that she had spotted his cousin.

But his mouth dropped open.

When he answered, uttering an affirmative

grunt, the cardiologist was already quickly moving in his cousin's direction.

"I guess that's a *yes*," Ellie commented to her sister.

Addie couldn't help the smile that curved her lips as she watched the two men hug one another with delighted enthusiasm.

"Certainly looks that way to me," Addie replied. Taking a closer look, she commented, "They almost look more like brothers than just cousins."

Ellie recalled what Neil had mentioned when he told her about Jason. "That probably has something to do with the fact that Neil and Jason's fathers were twins," she stated.

Addie laughed to herself. "I guess that there are just so many combinations of handsome genes that nature can come up with," she theorized.

Once the two cousins dropped their arms and stepped back, they immediately began talking practically nonstop.

Ellie had a feeling that the two men were just getting started. "What do you say we break this up, unless we're prepared to hang around all day and wait for that to happen naturally?" she asked her sister.

Addie was all for that. "Sounds good to me," she said, then gestured for Ellie to walk in front of her. "After you. Since you're the reason that Neil invited his cousin here in the first place."

Ordinarily Ellie might have protested that idea, but she was very eager to meet this cousin who was so important to Neil. She had a very strong feeling that if neither she nor Addie said anything, Neil and Jason could very well be at this for a very long time.

Ellie wanted to get Neil and his cousin back to Forever. She thought it was important that Jason was comfortable in his surroundings. The better feeling he got for the small town, the better chance of the hospital becoming a reality.

Allowing her instincts to take center stage, Ellie hurried over to meet the man who had been such a very important part of her fiancé's earlier life.

Ellie was about to introduce herself to Jason when, alerted by the look in Neil's eyes, Jason turned toward her, surmised her identity and extended a greeting first.

"You must be the woman who captured my cousin's heart." Smiling warmly, Jason covered Ellie's outstretched hand with both of his own. "I've got to say, his description doesn't begin to do you justice," he told her just before he shifted his eyes toward Addie. "And you must be her sister. I had no idea that beauty came in pairs."

Okay, so the man obviously saw himself as a smooth operator, Addie thought. She was not entirely comfortable with that.

"There's no need to flatter me," Addie told Jason in a rather abrupt manner. "Ellie already said yes to Neil and we've all welcomed him into the family. Besides, I've never had any influence over Ellie."

Jason looked somewhat amused. "Certainly speaks her mind, doesn't she?" he commented to his cousin.

Ellie was the one who answered him after shooting her sister a silencing look. "Always, I'm afraid," she sighed. "Even if her opinion might not be sought after, or even welcomed." Turning her head slightly, she mouthed to Addie, "Be nice."

"Sorry," Addie apologized, forcing the words to her lips. "I thought I was being nice."

She had gotten the distinct impression that Neil's cousin was talking down to her, as if he felt that if he poured on enough syrup, she would eagerly respond to empty flattery.

"C'mon, Jason," Neil said, clamping an arm around his cousin's shoulders. "Let's go get your luggage so we can be on our way. I can't wait for you to get your first look at the latest town where you're going to leave your mark." With that, Neil led his cousin over to the airport carousel, where a great deal of luggage was still merrily spinning around.

The moment Neil and his cousin went over to the luggage carousel, Ellie hung back and gave Addie a censoring look.

"What?" Addie asked, not entirely clear what that look was all about.

"What the heck's gotten into you?" Ellie asked, keeping her voice low so that neither Neil nor Jason could hear.

Addie shrugged dismissively, but she sensed that wouldn't be enough for her sister. With a sigh, she admitted, "Maybe I've had my fill of men who feel that they could turn a woman's head with just an insincere flattering word or two."

It was Ellie's turn to sigh. "Jason was just being nice," she told her sister. "You didn't need to bite his head off."

Addie was already beginning to cool off... and feel a little guilty about her reaction. "Maybe you're right."

"I know I'm right," Ellie told her sister flatly. "Lately, at times it feels as if you have this huge chip on your shoulder."

She was not about to stand around and be berated, especially not with Neil's cousin about to overhear their conversation at any minute. "You're imagining things, Ellie."

"I know you better than any person on the face of this earth," Ellie told her sister. "Now, out with it," she ordered. "Exactly what is it that's been bothering you?"

"Nothing," Addie insisted stubbornly.

There was no way on earth that she was about to tell her sister that what was bothering her was the fact that Neil and her nuptials were almost here. It had been all well and good when the date had been six months away. That allowed her to be happy for Ellie and her fiancé, and still not feel as if the big day was breathing down her neck, a clear signal that things were about to change—drastically—in her life. In essence, that meant that Ellie was no longer going to be part of her everyday life, the way she had been for all these years.

Moreover, her grandfather was apparently undergoing a life-altering change of his own, as well. If that had been the only thing going on at the moment, she felt she could be happy for him, even though she had to admit that she was also a little worried about the man.

But with all these changes taking place at the same time—or even apparently taking place at the same time—she didn't know how to handle them or even how to actually adjust to them.

The idea of feeling as if she was being left behind during what seemed to be a joyous occasion was selfish of her and Addie knew it, but at the same time, she just couldn't seem to help herself. Not to mention that she wasn't fooling Ellie.

"Nothing, my foot," Ellie responded, frowning at her sister.

Addie rolled her eyes at the phrase. "My lord, you're beginning to sound like some ancient married woman, Ellie. Just because you're going to be getting married in a week doesn't mean you have to start sounding as if you've been married since the beginning of time."

Ellie frowned. "Well, if you keep sounding like that, I'm going to have to start looking for another maid of honor to replace you, you know."

"No, you won't," Addie teased. "I'm irreplaceable."

As usual, her sister had managed to kid her out of her mindset, Addie thought, feeling in a somewhat better frame of mind. Maybe she was just being too sensitive about this whole situation and not really giving Jason a chance.

Out of the corner of her eye, Addie saw the

cousins heading back their way. They had divided Jason's luggage between them.

Addie tapped her sister's arm and nodded behind Ellie. "Looks like they found Jason's luggage and are on their way back."

Ellie took that as her cue to change the subject, at least for now.

"Why don't we table this conversation until later?" she suggested. Turning around to face Neil and his cousin, she asked the logical question. "Did you and Neil manage to find all of your luggage? A lot of times, people don't."

Jason nodded. "It's all here," he assured Ellie. He appreciated her asking and could easily see why Neil was attracted to her. "But then, I didn't pack all that much. Only one of the suitcases contains clothes. The other has reference material, my laptop and some software."

Addie looked surprised by his answer. "I thought you were planning on staying in Forever for a while."

"I am," Jason answered. "But that doesn't mean I need a lot of change of clothing," the builder assured both women. "Other than the photo that Neil sent me of the tuxedo he had picked out, all I needed to bring were a couple of pairs of jeans and a few work shirts. Plus one good suit, which I'm wearing."

That sounded like a rather laid-back approach, in Addie's opinion. Which meant that the man wasn't a peacock. She rather liked that. Maybe she *had* misjudged Neil's cousin, she thought.

Nodding her head, Addie commented, "Nice to hear."

Jason spared her a nod, then turned his attention to a far more interesting subject. He looked at his cousin's fiancée. "Neil told me that you fly your own plane."

"I do," Ellie answered. "The idea is for me to someday put together Forever's own airline."

Jason looked impressed. "That sounds very ambitious."

"Practical," Neil corrected his cousin proudly. "Ellie is exceptionally practical in her thinking."

Jason smiled warmly at his cousin's wife-to-be. "I'm really happy to know that Neil's in good hands," he told Ellie.

There was a sparkle in Neil's eyes as he looked at the woman who had completely captured his heart. "You'll get no argument from me." He slipped his free arm around Ellie's shoulders.

Jason observed the interaction between the couple. It pleased him to no end that Neil looked so happy and had finally found someone to spend his life with. Living in this little town wasn't the way he would have imagined Neil's life shaping up, but it obviously seemed to be working for his cousin.

Addie was standing off to the side, observing everything. She had taken to Neil practically from the very beginning. The cardiologist had saved Miss Joan's life and, on top of that, he hadn't even charged the woman. In her opinion, that made him an exceedingly generous man.

The way he treated her sister just served to confirm her opinion.

But if she was being honest, it was still too soon for her to form an actual opinion, one way or another, when it came to Neil's cousin…even though he seemed open to the idea of making the town's dream of building a hospital come true.

Yes, the man apparently seemed like the answer to a prayer, at least on paper. But before she was ready to throw Jason a parade to celebrate his presence in Forever, she wanted a little more to go on.

"Where is this plane of yours, Ellie?" Jason asked as they walked out of the airport with the sisters leading the way.

"Not too much farther," Ellie promised him. "Pilots park their private planes outside of the airport's perimeters."

"Don't worry," Neil told his cousin with a straight face. "Ellie can always find her plane. She drops bread crumbs."

"Sounds like an interesting method to keep track of something," Jason quipped.

"There it is," Addie said, pointing to it.

"*That's* your plane?" Jason asked, sounding slightly taken aback.

Thinking that Jason was being critical, Addie instantly took offense for her sister. Ellie had learned how to fly on that plane, and when the man who had taught her decided to sell his rather small airline, she had been more than eager to make the deal with him. She gave him her life savings and made arrangements to pay off the rest of the price in installments.

"It's a very sound plane," Addie informed him defensively. "My sister had it completely checked out before she purchased it, not that the man who had sold it to her would have attempted to cheat her. He was more than happy to know that his plane was getting a 'good home.'"

Ellie placed her hand on her sister's arm. "I'm sure that Jason didn't mean to imply anything else."

"I didn't," Jason quickly assured both sisters. "I just never met anyone who ever owned their own airplane."

"You'll have to forgive Jason," Neil said. "He's not used to independent women—or anyone out of his own field, actually. This is a whole new experience for him," he told Ellie and Addie, hoping to smooth over any potential rough spots. The last thing he wanted was for there to be waves created between them.

"No forgiveness necessary," Ellie said, then looked at her sister, waiting for Addie to agree. "Addie?"

Addie paused a moment, realizing that she was being touchy again. "Sorry," she murmured. "I guess I'm being overly protective."

"Addie has a tendency to bite people's heads off," Ellie explained.

"Don't apologize," Jason said. "I've never had anyone ride to my defense whenever I've said something that could be deemed questionable." His lips drew back into a smile. "It must be nice." He gestured toward the small passenger plane. "Okay, I think I'm sufficiently prepared. Show me around your plane," he said.

Chapter Three

"There's not all that much to see," Ellie told Neil's cousin as she brought Jason, Neil and Addie out to the plane. She ushered him and the others up the ramp. "Mainly the plane is predominantly meant to transport cargo and supplies. On occasion, such as now, passengers," she interjected. "But when I had to fly Miss Joan to the hospital, I was only able to bring her, Neil, who, of course, came as her doctor, and Miss Joan's husband. Trust me, that wasn't nearly everyone who wanted to be there for her or accompany her to the hospital."

Neil nodded, adding his voice to the scenario.

"That's one of the main reasons we want to build a hospital in Forever, so that the basic surgeries can be performed in town instead of fifty miles away…or farther," he said, thinking of where Miss Joan had been taken for her operation. "Fifty miles is all well and good if you have the time to spare to make a flight, but that isn't always the case," Neil pointed out.

Jason frowned slightly, looking uneasily around at the interior of the small plane. "I guess I've been spoiled," Jason confessed, directing his remark to the two Montenegro sisters. "Where I come from, getting to the nearest hospital doesn't require a pilgrimage. It doesn't even usually involve using up a tank of gas."

Ellie noticed that Neil's cousin was regarding the seats uneasily. She pointed toward them for Jason's benefit.

"Take your seats please and buckle up," Ellie directed. "We're going to be taking off as soon as you're ready."

Like an old pro, Neil sat down in the copilot seat next to Ellie. That left the remaining other two seats free for Addie and Jason.

Addie noticed that Jason looked a tad paler than he had a minute ago as he took the seat directly behind Neil. Leaning in toward the man, she did her best to reassure him. "Don't worry. Ellie's an old hand at this."

"I wasn't worried," Jason told her abruptly. Addie caught herself thinking that the builder didn't sound as if he was all that certain about what he was saying.

He looked even less so when Ellie began going through her initial countdown. The moment she did, because of its size, the plane started shaking and rumbling, creating a cacophony of noises as Ellie continued putting it through its paces.

Addie could feel rather than hear Jason catch his breath and he appeared more than a little concerned as he asked, "Is the plane all right?"

Because of the noise, he found he had to repeat the question in order for Addie to be able to make it out.

"You've never ridden in a small plane before, have you?" Addie asked.

Neil's cousin didn't answer. Instead, he shook his head from side to side as if verbalizing a response just made the plane's rumbling and shaking all that much more intense.

The fact that the noisy plane unsettled Jason managed to temporarily endear the man to her. The initial layers of his facade seemed to fall away and he didn't appear to be embarrassed by his display of nerves. His vulnerability made her smile.

She decided to let Jason see that he wasn't alone in his response. "The first time I heard that awful rattling sound," Addie told him, finding it necessary to talk directly in his ear in order for him to hear her above the loud din, "I was certain that the plane was going to just explode right then and there on the runway."

Because she felt it was important for him to pay attention to what she was telling him, Addie took hold of Jason's face in her hands. She turned it in her direction so he could make out what she had to say. She was worried that repeating herself might frustrate him.

"But it didn't explode," Addie pointed out to him.

Jason took a deep breath, doing his best to steady his nerves without appearing to do so. He liked to think of himself as being fearless, but he had to admit that this new experience challenged his preconceived notion of himself.

That was when he realized that the plane was climbing and he was clutching his armrests to the point that he was about to snap them off. To make matters worse, he saw that Addie was taking in his nervousness.

Jason drew in another deep breath and forced himself to release his grip on the armrests.

Addie's heart went out to the man. "It's okay," Addie assured him. "The seat can handle it. I can personally testify that the armrests are pretty flexible by now. I gave them a real workout the first dozen or so flights that Ellie took me on."

"You've flown with her a dozen times?" he marveled, looking at the petite woman sitting on the aisle seat next to him.

"I had to," she answered.

"Why?" It was the first question that occurred to him.

Well, she had come this far, Addie decided, so she might as well go all the way, even if this made her seem like she was vulnerable. "Because I had something to prove."

He still wasn't following her. He raised his voice. "And that was...?"

Her mouth curved. She was exposing herself and had to trust that he would take this in the spirit she was telling it to him.

"That I was just as brave as my sister. I felt that if I couldn't do that—if I couldn't handle that—I would never hear the end of it."

Jason looked at the back of Ellie's head, surprised. He couldn't make himself believe that his cousin's fiancée was like that.

"She'd actually taunt you with that?" he asked Addie.

"Oh, no, she wouldn't," Addie quickly answered. "But she wouldn't have to. I'd do it to myself."

More things that didn't make any sense to him, he thought. Jason shook his head. For the time being, the rattling plane was forgotten.

"Why would you do that?" he asked.

Addie laughed softly as she poked fun at herself. "Because I am the living embodiment of that very old song called 'Anything You Can Do (I Can Do Better)'—and if I couldn't do it better, at least I wasn't about to let it intimidate me," she told Jason, the corners of her mouth lifting even more.

For the first time since he had walked off his flight from New York, Jason looked at Neil's future sister-in-law. Really looked at her.

The young woman was something else again, he thought. Feisty, mercurial and pretty much in a class all by herself. Not to mention exceedingly pretty, Jason observed.

It was almost as if Addie was attempting to fight that concept, and went out of her way to dress down. In addition to that, she wasn't wearing any makeup on what was a near-perfect face.

What he saw, Jason mused, was apparently what he got…not that he minded that.

Watching the different expressions pass over the handsome builder's face, Addie put her own interpretation to them.

"Don't worry," she told him, raising her voice again. "We'll be landing in Forever before you know it," she assured Neil's cousin, "And then this—" she moved her hand around in a circular pattern to indicate the flight "—will all be over."

"I'm not worried," he told her.

"Okay," she replied, willing to go along with what the man was apparently trying to tell himself. For now, Addie decided that whatever got Neil's cousin through all of this with his integrity intact was all right with her.

Her decision actually surprised her, but this was for Ellie, not for her, Addie told herself. "But you'll still be happy to know that we'll be in Forever in less than thirty minutes. By the way," she added, "that includes from liftoff to landing."

If she was lying to him, he would definitely know, he thought, so she was probably telling him the truth.

Jason found himself greeting the news with more than a little relief.

He had never really been much of a flier. However, it really hadn't bothered him...until now. This experience was like sitting inside of a blender. A very noisy blender.

It wasn't as if his ears had been assaulted, but he felt that his insides had been completely shaken up.

Jason blew out a breath.

The trip was beginning to get to him again. He could feel it.

"Good to know," he acknowledged, referring to what she had said about how long the flight was going to last.

Jason was getting paler, Addie thought, growing concerned for him again.

"Focus on a pleasant memory," she urged. That had always worked for her. "And take deep breaths."

"I am," Jason snapped irritably.

This was a display of weakness, Addie assessed, and she could see that he wasn't happy about it. She forgave him, but right now, she had to pull him out of this tailspin he seemed to be in.

"Not deep enough to hyperventilate," she cautioned, continuing to describe how he should breathe, "just deep enough to take your mind off the fact that the plane is making more noise than a bunch of old-fashioned dental drills."

That just about covered the way he felt about the noise that was undulating all along—as well as under—his skin.

Jason discovered that he could handle the noise better if he didn't take his eyes off her face.

"Is that how you felt about the noise?" he asked, genuinely wanting to know.

"Absolutely," she answered with feeling.

Her response made him smile. "Did you tell your sister that?"

"Are you kidding?" she asked incredulously—and then she smiled. "No, at least not for a couple of years. Ellie loves this plane."

"What did she say when you did finally tell her that?" he asked.

Addie laughed softly under her breath. "Turns out that she knew."

Jason looked at the back of Ellie's head again, stunned. "She knew?"

Addie nodded. "There was never keeping anything from Ellie," she told Neil's cousin. "Even when we were kids. She could always figure things out. This time I think it might have had something to do with the fact that I was three shades lighter than a block of ice when I flew with her," she confided with a wink.

The wink seemed to go straight to the center of his stomach.

The image of Addie turning so very pale made Jason laugh, which in turn wound up making him relax a little.

At least relax enough to brace himself for the landing a few minutes later when Ellie brought the plane down right in front of what appeared to be a makeshift hangar.

It took him a minute to realize that he was still gripping Addie's hand to the point that her fingers were turning an interesting shade of purple.

Smiling at him patiently, Addie slowly uncoupled herself from his iron grip.

"We're here," Addie informed him, raising her voice so that Jason could hear her. "See, I told you we would be here before you knew it."

Surprise registered on his face as Ellie taxied her small passenger plane right into the transformed barn.

"Congratulations," Neil declared with genuine enthusiasm as he twisted around in his seat and looked at Jason. He undid his seat belt. "You've just had your first airplane ride on Ellie Airlines."

"You named the airline after yourself?" Jason asked Ellie as the plane slowly came to a halt.

"No, he did." Ellie nodded at Neil. "I wouldn't presume to name an airline—or a plane, actually—after myself."

Jason peered out the window on his side. "Is this an airplane hangar?" he asked. It certainly didn't look that way to him, but right now he was feeling very much like a fish out of water and he wasn't about to presume anything.

"No," Neil answered. "It's a converted barn. Addie and her grandfather built it. Someday, there'll be an actual airplane hangar built here, but since there's only one plane to house, this is going to have to do." He laughed affectionately, looking at the woman who was soon going to be his wife. "One small step at a time," he told his cousin. "Right now, setting up an actual hospital has taken the center stage in everyone's book."

They had discussed that already and Jason was looking forward to that being the next project that he tackled.

"I can understand that," Jason replied seriously.

The plane had stopped moving. Still feeling a little queasy, Jason gripped the armrests and rose to his feet quickly.

He regretted it immediately as he wavered a bit.

Standing right next to him, Addie saw that Jason looked as if he might actually wind up falling. She reacted quickly, propping her shoulder underneath his arm.

"Careful," she whispered with humor. "These small planes can throw you if you're not used to them."

He thought that was a rather silly sentiment to express, but before he could say as much, he felt his head start to spin. Jason swayed a little and caught his breath. He felt Addie's arm tighten around his waist.

"Better?" she asked, looking up at him brightly.

Realizing what was happening, Neil asked his cousin, "Are you okay?"

Addie cheerfully covered for Jason. "He's just getting his sea legs back."

They all knew that wasn't it, but for now that was enough of an excuse to cover for how wobbly his legs were.

Neil nodded understandingly. "My first few times were a little uncertain, too," he told Jason. "But you'll get used to it. By the time you leave here, you'll have trouble going back to flying on regular airplanes," he said.

Jason glanced at Addie before he tried his legs

again, gamely preparing to walk off the small plane. He slanted a look at his cousin.

"I sincerely doubt that," he commented.

"Oh, where's your faith?" Addie challenged.

"In the pit of my stomach, along with the rest of me," he whispered to her just before he walked behind Addie to get off the plane.

Holding on to the railing, Jason made his way down the makeshift ramp, moving far slower than he was happy about. But at this point, it was useless to attempt to prove anything to any one of these three people who had been on the plane with him. The last thing he wanted to do was take a chance on falling down in front of them.

He stopped at the bottom of the stairs, letting the wind travel over him and revitalize him for just a brief moment. It occurred to him that he had never felt quite so grateful to be upright and able to move before.

Obviously seeing the expression pass over Jason's face, Neil leaned over and confided, "Trust me, it'll get better from here on in."

Jason had no plan to conduct business by traveling back and forth from Forever and any other place while he was here. Whatever he thought he would need in order to complete setting up this hospital could be obtained via orders being placed and shipped to Forever. Technology, even in a place like Forever, had made great strides, or at least great enough to fulfill any order.

"I'm sure that it will," Jason answered his cousin.

He caught the amused expression on Ellie's sister's face.

The first indication he had that everything was going to work out and be all right was that he didn't bristle at the thought that there might be a problem…or that his situation seemed to be amusing her.

Jason felt himself starting to genuinely calm down.

Chapter Four

"I am very happy to finally meet you!" Eduardo said heartily, his large, capable hands all but swallowing up Jason's while introductions were made at the ranch house.

The girls' grandfather's words were warm as he quickly sized up Neil's cousin and found him to be exactly as Neil had described. "I hear that you are not only going to be Neil's best man, but I was also told that you are going to be responsible for bringing a much welcomed, much needed hospital to our little town."

There was genuine anticipation in Eduardo's

deep, resonant voice. He gestured for his visitor to be seated on the comfortable sofa in the living room.

"From what Neil told me, there was already a building in town that might suit our purposes perfectly," Jason replied. He was basing his response on what Neil had mentioned to him when they had discussed the idea of his working on a hospital in depth. "It just has to be renovated to some extent and, of course, the proper apparatus has to be purchased and installed."

Eduardo nodded, no doubt pleased that things were moving along in town and in his family.

"We have a professional contractor living here in Forever. She came here when the town decided it needed to have a small hotel on the premises. She remained after the job was over because, by then, one of the Murphy brothers had won her heart." Eduardo smiled fondly. "When the good doctor here began to talk about the possibility of a hospital coming to Forever, our contractor and Addie began to put their heads together."

The statement caught Jason totally off guard.

"Addie?" he echoed, surprised as he turned around to stare at the young woman who had just helped him overcome his uneasiness on the short flight to Forever.

Ellie grinned at Addie, guessing what had to have been going through Jason's head. "My sister is a woman of many talents," she told Neil's cousin.

Jason glanced at his cousin as he tried to wrap his mind around this newest piece of information. Nobody had mentioned to him that this feisty woman knew her way around power tools. He had thought that all the talk about helping to convert the barn into an airplane hangar had been just that—talk.

"You didn't really say anything about your future sister-in-law knowing what to actually *do* with a hammer and nails, or floor plans," Jason protested. Had he missed that somehow?

Neil shrugged. "I guess in all the excitement about the wedding and you agreeing to be my best man, *plus* agreeing to take on the hospital as your next project, I must have just forgotten"

Jason said nothing for the moment. He was still trying to picture Addie with tools in her hands. She looked as if she would be far more comfortable working on a ranch, something that he *did* remember Neil mentioning to him when they initially talked on the phone.

"Meanwhile," Ellie cheerfully said, "you have your choice of places to stay." She nodded at Jason's suitcases sitting on the floor next to the front door. "You can either stay with your cousin in what is going to be our future home after the wedding, or you can stay here on my grandfather's ranch."

Jason glanced at Addie before he forced himself to look elsewhere. "Well, I wouldn't want to impose," he protested.

The builder's usual mode of operation while he was working on projects was to camp out in hotel rooms. But the last project he had worked on had been close enough to his own home for him to stay there. This, however, would be completely different. And while the older man came across as very affable, Jason *had* arrived a week early with the sole intention of spending that week getting reacquainted with his cousin.

But then, it was a week before Neil's wedding and there had to be dozens of last-minute details for his cousin to see to.

There didn't seem to be a clear-cut answer to this dilemma no matter which way he turned.

"You are more than welcome here," Eduardo assured Jason. "I will not even make you brand any of the horses," he said, his eyes twinkling.

Neil could see the indecision on his cousin's face. "Tell you what," he began, "why don't we just leave your bags here for the time being and make the decision after we've taken you to meet Miss Joan and you've had something to eat?"

"Miss Joan," Jason repeated, looking at his cousin curiously as he tried to keep his facts straight. "That's the woman whose life you came out to save, right?"

"Oh, she's so much more than that," Neil told Jason with a laugh. "But you'll find that out for yourself soon enough."

This was starting to sound like one hell of a project he had agreed to take on. The work didn't seem like too much for him, but the people involved, like Addie and this Miss Joan, were something else altogether. For once in his life, he might have very well bitten off more than he had anticipated.

At the very least, he thought, this project would definitely not be run-of-the-mill, or boring.

Following Ellie, Addie and Neil, the very moment that Jason entered Miss Joan's Diner, he became aware of a wall of noise surrounding him. The wall of noise combined with incredible smells that seductively blended together in a tempting swirl. It did more than whet his appetite.

It vividly reminded him that because of a pressing schedule, he hadn't had a chance to eat anything of substance since late last night. Quite simply, he was really, really hungry.

Jason carefully made his way in through the rather interesting collection of humanity in this establishment.

Despite the number of people in the diner at this hour, Miss Joan was instantly aware of the doctor and his companions the very second that they walked in through the diner's front doors. Like an empress overseeing her domain, her eyes were immediately drawn toward them.

The woman's surgery had done nothing to dull her senses, Addie thought, as she noticed Miss Joan looking at them.

The woman's bright hazel eyes were all but weighing and absorbing Jason, who had walked in beside Neil, the cardiologist she credited for saving her life.

The expression on the diner owner's face was issuing a greeting to Neil's cousin even before he had crossed the floor to the counter.

Always keenly aware of all her surroundings, Miss Joan continued eying Jason. "So this is the young man who is going to finally bring the twenty-first century to Forever," she declared with a knowing nod of her head. The slightest smile curved her mouth. "I'd say it was about time, wouldn't you?"

It was a rhetorical question addressed to the diner patrons in general. She was not expecting any sort of a debate or even an actual answer.

"Plant yourselves at any table you find," Miss Joan ordered, gesturing around the diner.

Addie looked around the crowded place. "That might be a little more difficult than it sounds," she predicted to the threesome with her.

The words were no sooner out of the young woman's mouth than Miss Joan glared sharply at the occupants of several of the tables located closest to her. At least two of the tables had one remaining occupant each. Another had two.

Rather than walk across the floor, Miss Joan projected her voice and announced, "You, Jake, you're about done. So are you, Damon and Rose." In both cases, it a question, not a statement. "Why don't you either join forces, or finish up at the counter? I need a table for four," she announced.

When no one appeared to be gathering their things together, Miss Joan added firmly, "I mean today."

Instantly, two of the tables were cleared and a third table followed.

"That's more like it," Miss Joan said, nodding

her approval. She looked over toward the four-some who had just walked into her diner. "As I said—" the matriarch gestured at the vacated tables "—take your pick. Just let Iris know which one you like so that she can clear the dishes away and clean up for you."

Impressed by the woman's take-charge attitude, Jason leaned in toward his cousin. "Is she always like this?" he whispered.

Addie was the one who answered him. "No, this is one of Miss Joan's laid-back days."

"And I'll have you know that there's nothing wrong with my hearing, Builder Boy," Miss Joan informed him. "It was my heart your cousin fixed, not my ears." She got back to the business at hand. "Find a table to your liking yet?"

Since Jason felt she was directing the question toward him, he selected the table closest to the rear of the diner. It gave the impression of some sort of privacy. "That one?"

Miss Joan arched a carefully penciled-in eye-brow. "Are you asking me or telling me?"

Jason squared his shoulders. This was no time to act as if the woman was intimidating him. Once she thought that, he had a feeling it would be downhill from there.

"Telling you, ma'am," Jason added.

She nodded, approving his respectful response. "Good choice." She turned toward the waitress at her side. "You heard him, Iris, Builder Boy likes that one." She pointed toward the table Jason had selected.

Nodding at Jason, signaling a temporary end to their exchange, Miss Joan turned back to a customer who was waiting patiently at the register and gave him his receipt.

Jason released a breath as he stepped back, allowing the woman Miss Joan had called Iris to clear off the table and prepare it for them.

"So that's the famous Miss Joan," he whispered to his cousin.

Neil smiled broadly. "Yeah, that's her, all right."

Hearing the exchange, Addie added in her two cents for Jason's benefit. "She takes a little getting used to," she confided, her expression matching Neil's.

"Does a shot of whiskey help matters any?" Jason asked a bit cryptically.

"It can if you stop in at Murphy's," Ellie told her fiancé's cousin.

"Murphy's?" Jason repeated, unfamiliar with the name.

"That's the town's bar," Ellie explained.

That brought up a whole new question. "The

town only has one bar?" Jason asked. That seemed a bit austere, he thought. Wouldn't a town like this have at least several bars, even if it was a small town?

Addie stepped up to answer the question. "Miss Joan and the Murphys made an arrangement a long time ago. The Murphys don't serve food with their drinks, except peanuts and chips, and Miss Joan doesn't serve any hard liquor with her meals. That way, no toes get stepped on and everything remains nice and friendly," she explained.

At that point, Iris finished clearing away the remaining dishes and then ran a damp cloth over the tabletop. She indicated to the foursome that they could now come over and sit down.

"And nobody ever crosses the line?" Jason asked, clearly surprised.

"Nobody has so far," Ellie replied.

Addie's eyes danced with amusement. "Would you?" she asked him. "We're talking about offending *Miss Joan*," she said with emphasis. "That just isn't done."

With that, they all took their seats at the freshly cleaned table. Iris faded into the background as another young, equally lively-looking server, with a name tag that read Dolores, stepped forward and handed them their menus.

Unlike the menus he had occasionally picked up in some of the diners he intermittently frequented, Jason noted that this one, along with the other three menus, appeared to be newly cleaned. He wondered if that was by accident, or if it was deliberate.

He looked over the menu he had in his hand. "What is she, the town dictator?" Jason asked, unable to help himself.

"Not a dictator," Addie answered. "More like a beloved despot," she said just as Dolores returned with four tall glasses of water with small, delicate shards of ice clinking around in the glasses.

Jason raised his eyes to look at his cousin in disbelief, but Neil didn't appear as if the statement about Miss Joan being a beloved despot challenged his common sense.

Jason eyed the water glasses suspiciously. "Something in the water?" he asked, only partially kidding.

"Nope, just pure spring water," Dolores replied, overhearing the question.

Jason didn't respond to her. He just smiled, but he still moved the glass off to the side.

"You'll have to forgive my cousin," Neil apologized to his future wife and her sister. "Jason has always been a bit of a skeptic," he told them.

"He doesn't trust fire until he can pass his fingers through the flames and feel the heat himself."

Rather than appear offended for Miss Joan the way Ellie thought her sister would, Addie looked rather amused by the whole thing. "This is going to be a really interesting wedding."

His eyes met Addie's and Jason smiled. "Well, I'm always open to new experiences," Jason told her.

"Then brace yourself for one really unsettling roller-coaster ride," Ellie said.

Jason continued to smile. He was not about to contradict his cousin's bride-to-be. In his opinion, the people in this small town really needed to get out more and experience things on a somewhat grander scale. But he was here for Neil's wedding and, after that, to help these people turn an old, wayward building into something far more useful than a collection of former barns and stables.

After asking a few questions, he'd found out that the land was going to be razed and then the entire area renovated. At that point, it would be turned into a modern-looking hospital with state-of-the-art X-ray machines, equipment for EEGs and EKGs and a collection of laboratories, all of which would be immensely beneficial to the residents of Forever.

"Are you ready to order?" the server asked Jason.

Thoughts about Miss Joan and everything else associated with this new project that he would face after the wedding was over quickly faded into the background.

Before Jason could speak up to answer Dolores, his stomach did. It made noises to assert just how very hungry it actually felt.

"I think that's a *yes*," Neil confirmed for his cousin just before he laughed. The others all joined in.

Chapter Five

Because he felt extremely hungry, Jason went ahead and ordered a sirloin steak. He ordered it despite the fact that he had his doubts about how good it would be at a diner located in the middle of nowhere.

His expectations were rather low, but then again, the hunger he felt was on the high side. He thought that at the very least, what he ordered would fill the gnawing emptiness in his stomach to some extent.

When the food arrived, Jason regarded his plate for a long moment before finally cutting into his steak. After taking a breath, he slipped a small bite into his mouth, fervently hoping he wouldn't wind up regretting having ordered it.

His lips closed around that first piece, then he slowly chewed and swallowed it. Jason was certain that he was imagining the taste that he thought was bursting out on his tongue. So he took another tentative bite of the steak and swallowed it.

And then another.

As each bite registered, his eyes widened more and more.

Addie was sitting opposite Neil's cousin and watched his face, completely fascinated. She wasn't sure just how to interpret his expressions, although she had her suspicions.

He seemed totally stunned.

Having come to the diner for most of her young life, she played innocent. "Something wrong?" she asked Jason.

He raised his eyes to her face, then looked back at his plate.

"Yes," he replied almost in slow motion, "I think I'm hallucinating." Jason still wasn't sure that the steak he had sampled was registering correctly.

To make sure there wasn't anything drastically off with his taste buds—oncoming colds could do that—Jason skimmed just a little of the mashed potatoes onto his fork and sampled them. To his surprise, the forkful tasted fine. Better than fine. The mashed potatoes he'd just had reminded him of the ones he'd had at several high-end restaurants in New York City.

Amused by his cousin's look of disbelief, Neil asked, "How's that hallucination of yours coming along?"

Jason shook his head in bewilderment like a man attempting to emerge from a dream. Then, finally, he surrendered to the truth.

"This is actually good," he murmured in absolute wonder.

"Oh, good," Addie declared with a straight face. "Then the hypnosis is working."

Jason did a double take before he realized that she was pulling his leg.

Ellie stifled a laugh. Taking pity on Neil's cousin, she told him truthfully, "The food here is beyond good. That's why Miss Joan's place is always so packed, no matter what time of day or evening it might be. Miss Joan makes sure that she employs only the best people preparing food for her customers. She cares too much for the people frequenting her diner to ever consider shortchanging them."

"But I saw the prices," Jason argued. "They certainly don't reflect anything out of the ordinary."

"They wouldn't have to," Ellie told him, doing her best not to laugh at the bewildered expression on the builder's face. "Charging a lot for something doesn't necessarily mean that it has to be good, just overpriced."

"Besides," Addie added, "the people who work here feel that they owe it to Miss Joan to do a good job. Over the years, she has taken in a lot of the residents who work here, given them jobs, trained them when they had absolutely no idea how to even boil water.

"Taking a chance on them has paid off well for her," Addie continued. She glanced over her shoulder toward the counter and Miss Joan. She could remember a time when she was a little girl and Miss Joan's stern demeanor frightened her. "If you don't know her, Miss Joan can be a very scary lady," she admitted.

Ellie laughed. "Sometimes, even if you *do* know her, she can still be a very scary lady. But under that dark, intimidating expression there beats a heart of pure gold." Then to emphasize her words, Ellie crossed her heart and solemnly said, "I promise."

Jason still had his doubts about what he was hearing, but he knew what he liked.

"Well, I don't know about the heart-of-gold part," he said as he continued eating, "but this food certainly is surprisingly good."

"That would probably be thanks to Angel," Addie told him as she forked up a piece of chicken Parmesan from her own plate.

"Angel?" Jason echoed, scanning the table for an explanation. He assumed Addie wasn't being literal, although when it came to this town, he was beginning to believe that he couldn't take too much for granted. Things apparently weren't always what they seemed.

"Angel Rodriguez," Ellie told Jason, volunteering the diner's best chef's name. She gave him some of the woman's background, a story she and her sister had always found fascinating. "She's the deputy sheriff's wife now, but when Gabe first found her, two of her car's wheels were hanging off a cliff. Through a heroic effort, Gabe managed to save her life, but it was really touch-and-go at the time.

"Someone had run into her—on purpose, it turned out—and she had hit her head in the accident. When she came to, she had amnesia."

"That's why he called her Angel," Addie interjected.

"It was a slow road to recovery," Ellie continued. "But part of that road did involve her getting a job at the diner, where she discovered, totally by accident, that she had a wonderful gift for cooking."

Addie picked up the story. "When she finally did recover her memory, again completely by accident, she decided that she wanted to stay in Forever for the long haul—with Gabe," she concluded, then smiled. "So far, they're doing very, very well and are well on their way to living happily ever after."

"Well, if her cooking is any indication of how she's doing," Jason said, "I totally agree. But I really have to admit that I'm surprised to find this kind of cooking out here. I thought food was just something people ate to survive, not for pleasure."

"Why, Builder Boy?" Miss Joan asked.

The sound of Miss Joan's voice made Jason jump.

"Did you expect to find us living on mud pies and trying our best not to throw up?" Miss Joan asked. Circling around to face Jason, she looked at the man archly, waiting for a response.

"He meant no disrespect, Miss Joan," Neil quickly explained, coming to his cousin's defense.

"Sometimes he has a little trouble remembering that New York City isn't the last word in civilization."

Miss Joan nodded solemnly, as if taking Neil's words into consideration.

"Well, since he's your cousin and he *has* come out here to work on Forever's first hospital, as well as being your best man—" the expression on Miss Joan's face indicated that she found that description rather amusing "—I'll let him slide." She fixed Jason with a look. "This time," Miss Joan added with a warning look. "But don't get used to it."

The woman looked around at the other three people seated at the table. "Everything taste all right?" Miss Joan asked.

"Everything is excellent as always, Miss Joan," Neil quickly told her.

"Delicious," Ellie assured the woman.

"It's why I keep coming back," Addie said to the town matriarch.

The woman nodded—the expression on her face testified that she had expected nothing less, but was just checking.

A small smile curved her thin lips. "The meal is on me. Enjoy yourselves and take your time." Then, just before she turned on her heel and left, she told the foursome, "I'll see you all at the church next week."

Neil looked over at his cousin's face and chuckled. "The woman certainly is something else, isn't she?" There was unabashed humor shining in his eyes.

It took a moment for Jason to draw his eyes away from the woman's back as she walked away and focus on the others at the table. "To say the very least," Jason agreed.

"She might seem abrasive," Neil told Jason, "but like Ellie said, the woman really does have a heart of gold. Anyone who's ever found themselves in trouble, or fallen on hard times, knows that they could turn to Miss Joan for help. She *always* comes through for people, although not exactly the way they might have initially anticipated."

Jason shrugged, not completely convinced. But his cousin knew the woman far better than he did.

"I'll take your word for it," Jason said loftily.

"Well, until you need to do otherwise," Addie agreed, seemingly amused at his wording, "I'll guess you'll have to do just that."

Jason had the distinct impression that somewhere, a bell had rung and that he and Addie had returned to their respective corners to wait for the next round.

Turning his attention to his plate, Jason went back to eating the remainder of his meal. They moved on to a different subject.

Neil and Jason spent as much time as they could catching up on the last six months, just the way that the two cousins had hoped they could. There had been a time when they had all but lived in each other's back pockets, but they—and life— had moved on.

Still, they did what they could in the very limited time they had.

The hospital project was pushed into the background until after the wedding took place.

Both Neil and Ellie felt as if too much time had gone by already, although it was something they had agreed to voluntarily. They had felt that the wedding taking place without having Miss Joan as an integral part of every aspect of it would not have meant as much.

"You know, what if Miss Joan doesn't really feel up to organizing this wedding?" Ellie asked. "I mean, we did postpone the wedding for six months and at the time, it did seem doable, but that was because it was all those months away. But now it's less than a week away and she still hasn't said anything," she said to Neil as they sat in her grandfather's living room. "Granted, we have the wedding dress and the maid-of-honor dress, not to mention your tuxedo and Jason's—"

"And the reception is being held at Murphy's. The brothers are all on board," Addie pointed out, walking in on the discussion. "There's really not that much to do except calm down your butterflies and get Miss Joan's input."

"But I'd hate to put her on the spot if she's not up to it," Ellie said. "We don't want to take a chance on taxing her too much. She's not twenty anymore."

"Still, not asking the woman would really offend her," Neil said.

"Why do you not just have her tell you if she is up to it?" Eduardo suggested, joining the gathering.

"We were just trying to decide the best approach, Grandpa," Ellie told him as she turned around to look at the man.

"As usual, she has taken that matter out of your hands," he told his granddaughter and her fiancé. "Miss Joan has just called to say that she wants to see the four of you about the wedding tomorrow morning."

Ellie frowned slightly. "This is four days before the wedding," she said. "Isn't this cutting things a little close? Maybe this heart surgery took more out of her than she wants to admit. Maybe she's going to tell us to do what we want, and that she's not up to organizing our lives the way she used to"

Addie looked at her sister dubiously. "Does that really sound like Miss Joan to you?"

"I don't want to believe that, but—" Ellie began only to be cut short by her sister.

"Then don't," Addie told her. "Among other things, Miss Joan has always loved the dramatic effect. This is just part of that."

Eduardo shook his head. "If Miss Joan was not up to this, she would have handed the matter over to Zelda."

"I don't know, Grandpa. That would be rather hard for Miss Joan. She and her sister have made up to a great extent, but this would be like Miss Joan handing over her scepter to her sister, proclaiming her to be the next in line," Ellie said. "I'm not sure Miss Joan is ready to do that just yet."

"Maybe instead of debating whether or not she is or isn't ready to retire or go ahead with her end of the wedding preparations, wouldn't it just be easier on everyone all around if you just stop second-guessing what's on the woman's mind and ask her?" Jason suggested, looking from his cousin to Ellie. For his part, he had had to deal with difficult clients himself, and when he did, he had always just gone to the source.

"And that's why," Neil declared with a smile, "my cousin is such a great project manager. He cuts through the speculation and just gets to the heart of the matter." He looked at Ellie. "We'll go tomorrow and beard the lion in her den."

"I would suggest that if you want to go on living, you do not put it that way when you go talk to Miss Joan," Eduardo told them with an amused chuckle.

Ellie kissed her grandfather's cheek affectionately. "Right as always, Grandpa. Would you like to come with us?" she suggested. "She always liked you."

"True," Eduardo agreed, "but right now there is a slight stumbling block in the way."

"You mean Zelda?" Ellie guessed, remembering that the man seemed to be spending more and more time with Miss Joan's sister lately.

Eduardo nodded. He saw no reason to pretend things were otherwise. In all the years he had been taking care of his granddaughters, he had been completely devoted to them. But things had taken a slightly different turn in the last few months.

"Sad as it is to admit," he answered, "I mean Zelda."

"So your Miss Joan is that small-minded?" Jason asked. He supposed that would explain a lot, at least to him.

"She's trying *not* to be that small-minded," Addie said, speaking up and coming to Miss Joan's defense. "Don't forget, I told you that Miss Joan's sister had put her through a lot. They are trying to put the past behind them, especially Miss Joan, but it isn't always that easy, good intentions or no good intentions."

Ellie took in a deep breath as if bracing herself. Whatever there was for Neil and her to face, the sooner they did it, the better. She knew that in both of their opinions, they had already waited far too long. If this meant that what they had done was to benefit the woman everyone loved, all well and good. But if it turned out that they had just waited too long for no reason, they needed to find out right now before any more time went by.

"Are you ready to see her tomorrow?" she asked Neil.

He smiled at the woman he had fallen head over heels in love with. "I was ready the day you flew me into Forever," Neil told her. "I just didn't know it at the time."

Ellie nodded. "Good answer."

Chapter Six

The following morning, Ellie and Neil, as well as Addie and Jason, all went into town to see Miss Joan at the diner. Neil was the one who called her, and it was agreed that she would discuss the wedding arrangements with them just after the breakfast crowd had more or less dispersed.

Jason looked around the diner as they walked in. "I guess this place isn't always stuffed to the gills." He had come away with the impression earlier that the diner was always filled.

"It's in between shifts," Addie told him just before Miss Joan came forward.

A joint chorus of "Hello" was the last word that any of them were able to say before Miss Joan took over.

The woman turned to look at her main morning server. "Take over, Dolores," she instructed, waving her hand toward the few customers who still remained in the diner. "I have wedding business to discuss with these good people." Miss Joan paused and glanced at Jason before she pursed her lips and amended, "Well, mostly good people." She hadn't seemed to have quite made up her mind about Jason yet.

Gesturing for the foursome to follow her to the back booth, Miss Joan instructed, "This way."

"If you ask me," Jason murmured under his breath to Addie, "the woman has fully recovered from her surgery and is definitely back to her sunny old self."

Addie threw him a glance. He was being sarcastic and she didn't know if she liked that or not.

"But you didn't know her before this," she pointed out.

"From what I've managed to pick up, I can make an educated guess." He followed Addie to the booth behind Neil and Ellie.

"Take a seat," Miss Joan told the group. Raising her hand, she signaled for Dolores to take an order. When the woman arrived at the booth, she told her, "Bring them four coffees and four sweet rolls, please."

That was the last verbal exchange between Miss Joan and anyone else. For the next half hour, Miss Joan did all the talking. She laid out all the wedding arrangements, including the time that the ceremony would begin, as well as any and all details involved, from the large to the minute. Miss Joan was nothing if not extremely precise.

And when she was finally finished, the diner owner rose to her feet a little more slowly than she was happy about. She scanned the faces of the four people in the booth.

"Any questions?" she asked, presuming that there wouldn't be any. When she was proven right and no one spoke up, she nodded. "I didn't think so. But if you do happen to come up with anything, you know where to find me," she told them. "Meanwhile, someone has to run this place." And with that, Miss Joan returned to the front of the diner.

Jason laughed softly as he finished the last of his sweet roll. "That woman definitely needs to have her own country to rule," he commented, dusting off his fingers with a napkin.

Addie raised her eyes to his. "What makes you think that she doesn't already have one?"

Jason allowed an amused smile to play on his lips. "Good point," he said, inclining his head. He glanced over toward his cousin for some sort of confirmation, or denial, regarding Addie's comment.

But Neil had slipped his hand over Ellie's and, judging from the expression on both their faces, it appeared as if the duo had gone off into a world of their own making.

He laughed under his breath. "Well, it looks like they're really excited about the big day," he commented to Addie.

Jason finished the last of his coffee.

Addie got a kick out of the builder's simple observation. "And just what was your first clue?" she asked.

"I've always been intuitive that way," Jason answered.

It was at that point that she decided that there just might be hope for Neil's cousin yet. It also made her think that there was a strong possibility that working with the man on the hospital might not be as bad as she had anticipated.

After Neil had proposed to Ellie, waiting for Miss Joan to heal for the wedding day had felt like one long, endless proposition.

In comparison, after all the arrangements were

finally set, the next four days seemed as if they just flew by, evaporating before they even took form.

And then, suddenly, the big day finally arrived.

The night before, Ellie hardly slept at all and was waking up every few minutes. She finally gave up all attempts at finding any restful sleep. Surrendering, she threw off her covers sometime around seven.

She had no recollection of showering or eating. The next few hours, until she was standing in front of her wedding gown, were all a blur.

And then, putting on her wedding gown, Ellie felt as if she was literally all thumbs.

When she failed to tuck a button through a loop for the third time, for one of the very first times in her life, a frustrated curse escaped her lips.

Peeking into her sister's room to see what was responsible for causing this uncharacteristic display of temper, Addie immediately saw Ellie's dilemma.

The moment Ellie felt Addie's fingers pushing hers out of the way and taking over, buttoning the row of buttons marching up her back, Ellie sighed her relief.

"Thanks," she murmured, her eyes meeting Addie's in the mirror above the bureau. "Funny, I thought I'd be calmer than this."

Even now, it was all she could do to keep her hands from shaking.

"Funny, I thought you'd be more nervous than this," Addie joked as she swiftly completed buttoning the tiny row of pearl buttons.

"Wait," Ellie said as she pressed her hand against her queasy stomach. Breakfast had been a mistake, she now realized. "We haven't left the house yet."

Addie laughed. "Don't worry, El," she said, rubbing a comforting hand along her sister's shoulder, "when we do, the sky's not going to fall."

"There's a lot more of the day to go," Ellie said, not taking any comfort in her sister's prophecy.

Addie met her sister's eyes in the mirror again. She had never seen Ellie looking quite this pale. The poor thing really was nervous, Addie thought.

"Breathe, Ellie, breathe," she told her sister. "Before you know it, this will all be a just a beautiful distant memory. Want my advice?" she asked, then told her, "Just enjoy it while you can."

Ellie turned her head slightly, a surprised look registering on her freshly made-up face.

"When did you get to be so wise-sounding?" she asked.

"Oh, I guess I didn't tell you, did I?" Addie said, doing what she could to keep a straight face. "When she wasn't paying attention, I've been taking in all the pearls of wisdom my sister has uttered over the years. I secretly managed to pick up some real gems while I was at it."

Ellie started to laugh, holding up her hand to make her sister stop. "You make me laugh and pop a button on this thing, and I'll never forgive you," she warned Addie.

Addie's smile widened as her eyes sparkled. "Duly noted, big sister."

At that moment, there was a very light knock on Ellie's bedroom door. Both young women looked toward it and uttered in unison, "Come on in, Grandpa."

Opening the door slowly—just in case they weren't ready—Eduardo peered into the room. He appeared solemn, as if he was torn between overwhelming happiness and the sort of deep sentimentality that brought tears to a man's eyes.

"It's time, girls," he said. And then as if taking in the scene for the first time, Eduardo looked from one granddaughter to the other. He sighed wistfully. "I guess you are not girls anymore. I should have called you 'ladies.'"

Ellie impulsively hugged the man on one side while Addie hugged him at the same time on the other.

"We will *always* be your girls, Grandpa," Addie promised.

Eduardo smiled warmly, allowing himself a moment just to drink in this display of affection. His gray eyes crinkled as he looked from one granddaughter to the other. It was really hard for him to believe that they had grown so much and were now such beautiful young women, but they clearly were.

"That is very good to know," Eduardo responded with feeling. "But we still need to get to the church," he pointed out, seeking refuge in pragmatism. "And the time is growing short."

Addie picked up her sister's train, carefully tucking the material against her chest to keep the lace from dragging along the ground.

"Lead the way to your car, Grandpa," she urged.

Turning on his heel, Eduardo gladly did just that.

It seemed like all of Forever had turned up at the church to witness Ellie and Neil's wedding ceremony. It was obvious that there wasn't room for everyone inside the building, so latecomers wound up spilling out the doors onto the grounds outside. The doors were left open so that everyone outside could hear the words being spoken, thanks to the loudspeakers that the Murphy brothers had provided for just this occasion.

"Are you all right, baby?" Eduardo asked Ellie, concerned, just as he and his granddaughter approached the door of the church.

"Never better," Ellie assured her grandfather breathlessly. She flashed a smile at him as he tucked her arm through the crook in his and gave it a reassuring pat.

"You do know that your hands are freezing," her grandfather pointed out.

"I know. But they'll warm up," Ellie replied with a smile she hoped wasn't quivering.

Addie grinned at her sister. "I know one way to get your hands warm," she whispered in Ellie's ear. Ellie swatted at her.

"Girls."

When they both looked at him, Eduardo called his granddaughters' attention toward the front of the church.

Addie took her cue. "I'm going, Grandpa," she told him, then began to make her way up to the front of the altar.

As soon as Addie started moving, Ellie took another deep breath, then, fortified, she nodded toward her grandfather.

They started to rhythmically move right behind Addie.

Ellie's eyes were on Neil with each step she took. Cutting the distance between them, she was hardly aware of even moving her feet. Her heart was pounding wildly and joyfully. Her hands were no longer so icy cold.

The closer she drew, the less cold her hands felt.

And then she felt her grandfather's arm slip away from hers.

Just before Eduardo took a step back, he brushed his lips against her cheek. "Be happy," he whispered to Ellie.

Addie took the bouquet out of her sister's hands. Ellie was hardly aware that any of this was happening. Her attention was totally focused on the man who was about to become her husband.

As Ellie took her position next to Neil, he smiled at her and said softly, "I've been waiting for you my whole life."

Addie felt her heart swell as she watched Neil and her sister stand in front of the preacher. Someday, if she was lucky, she would find someone like that herself, she thought.

For some reason, as that thought went through her head, Addie caught herself glancing over toward Jason.

Oddly enough, he had picked that exact moment to look over toward her.

And smile.

She had no idea why, but it felt as if there was an electrical charge all but crackling through the air.

Addie looked back at the couple in front of the preacher and upbraided herself to pay attention.

"You know, considering how long you and I have been waiting to finally have that ceremony take place, it felt as if it just went whizzing by," Neil confided to his brand-new wife.

Ellie was in his arms at Murphy's and they were dancing their very first dance as husband and wife. Everything felt as if it was absolutely glowing around them. Ellie hardly felt the floor beneath her feet.

She laughed softly. "I think that's because everyone wanted to get to Murphy's so they could toast us and start in on the feast that Miss Joan brought. It looks like a really nice spread," Ellie commented.

This was one of those rare occasions when Miss Joan and the Murphys joined together and combined their efforts.

"I wouldn't know," Neil told her as he whirled her around the floor. "I only have eyes for you."

Ellie's smile rose all the way up into her eyes.

"Remember that years from now," she told her new husband.

"I will," Neil promised.

Coming up behind Addie, who was seated at the table, Jason bent his head so that she could hear him above the din.

"Would you like to dance?" he asked the maid of honor. "I think we're allowed to now."

Addie looked up the best man, surprised that he had asked her. He hadn't struck her as the type who liked to dance and this wasn't exactly a conventional wedding that went by the rules. Rising, Addie turned toward Neil's cousin and presented her hands to him.

"As a matter of fact, yes, I would."

"Then let's get to it, shall we?" Jason said warmly.

Addie braced herself, not knowing exactly what she was leaving herself open for. Admittedly, she wasn't expecting very much. As a matter of fact, she half expected that Jason would be a clumsy dancer and would wind up stepping on her toes. Since this was Ellie's special day, Addie felt she could handle it.

When Neil's cousin enfolded her in his arms and began to gently sway with the music, she was pleasantly surprised. She was even more surprised when Jason held her closer to him. A wave of warmth radiated through her.

Suddenly, it was as if they had always been this close, always moving together in rhythm. She didn't bother to hide her shock or even try to explore the feeling.

"You dance very well," she told Jason.

He looked down into her face, amused. "Not quite the clod you thought I was?"

"I never thought you were a clod," she replied. "I just didn't think that dancing was very high up on your list of things to conquer."

He laughed then as he suddenly executed a dramatic turn, whirling Addie around on the floor.

"Did I say something funny?" she asked.

"Only if you knew nothing about my mother," he told her.

"I'm going to need more of a hint than that," Addie replied.

He leaned his cheek against Addie's hair, taking in a deep breath. *Heady stuff*, he caught himself thinking.

"My mother always required excellence in everything. 'If you're going to do something, Jason, make sure you do it well,'" he said in a high voice that Addie assumed he meant to sound like his mother.

"Are you an only child?" Addie asked him, curious. If she had bet money, she would have said that he was.

Jason nodded. "Totally and utterly."

She was beginning to understand why he and Neil had been so close as boys. Neil had undoubtedly been his cousin's support system.

At another table, Zelda approached Eduardo. "You need to smile," she told him. "This is a happy time." Moving in front of the bride's grandfather, she lifted up her arms toward him in a silent invitation. "If you're not busy or spoken for, I would like this dance, please."

His granddaughters had always been somewhat outspoken, but he wasn't quite certain how to react to that trait in someone else. He looked a little uncertainly at Miss Joan's sister. "Are you sure?"

"I'm sure," she answered. "These days, I never say anything I don't mean. I learned that little lesson the hard way from Joan."

Eduardo nodded his head. "All right, if you think you are up for it."

She smiled brightly up into his eyes and told him with conviction, "I am."

With that, Zelda, who barely came up to the man's shoulder, began to lead him toward the dance floor.

Chapter Seven

Addie slowly opened her eyes, trying to orient herself.

It was Monday morning.

The long-awaited wedding was now part of history.

The house felt oddly empty.

There had been many times when Ellie had been away on a trip, or just out of town for a week. During those days, Addie would pass her sister's room, noting how empty it was.

But this was decidedly different.

Now it wasn't just an empty room. This time Ellie was gone, starting a new chapter of her life. While it was true that she couldn't be happier for her sister, that still didn't make the emptiness fade away.

Addie threw off the covers and went to the bathroom to start getting ready.

"If you feel this way," she said to the reflection in her bathroom mirror, "think about how Grandpa must feel." If nothing else, the poor man had to be going through a partially empty-nest syndrome… and she wasn't going to be around to help. She and Jason had agreed to get started working on the proposed hospital as soon as the happy couple had gone off on their honeymoon.

That meant that she would be working in town for most of the time.

Her heart ached for her grandfather. Oh, she knew he still had the horses to tend to and he did have Luke and Phil, his longtime ranch hands, to help out. They lived in the bunkhouse, but even so, Addie didn't think that would help the older man fill the void that had suddenly opened up in his life.

She looked herself over in the mirror. She certainly wasn't doing her grandfather any favors just standing up here.

After going back into her room, Addie threw on a pair of jeans and a work shirt. She wasn't trying to impress anyone, she told herself, thinking of Jason. She was just dressing for work.

Taking one last quick critical look in the mirror, she quickly hurried down the stairs to the kitchen.

From the sounds she heard as she came to the bottom, her grandfather was already up.

Poor man probably didn't get any sleep. Most likely her grandfather probably spent the night looking over pictures from when she and Ellie and were little girls and had come to live with him.

Addie wasn't usually happy-go-lucky first thing in the morning, but she was determined to make an effort *this* morning for her grandfather.

"Hi, Grandpa!" she called out cheerfully as she crossed the threshold into the kitchen. Addie sported a wide smile on her face. "Did you get a good night's sleep?"

"As a matter of fact, I did," he answered as he turned away from the stove to look in her direction. "I slept very soundly. So soundly," he admitted with an embarrassed, almost self-deprecating chuckle, "that I almost overslept."

She didn't understand. "Overslept?" she echoed. "Overslept what? Luke and Phil are here to take care of the horses. You don't have to do anything if you don't want to, Grandpa."

"I was not worried about the horses," he told her. "I did not want you starting your first day on the new hospital on an empty stomach."

Saying that, Eduardo emptied the contents of the frying pan onto a plate, then brought it, and a steaming cup of coffee, over to the table.

Addie waved aside his concern. "I could always swing by Miss Joan's diner if I suddenly felt hungry," she reminded him. It wasn't as if she would suddenly starve.

Eduardo frowned at her. "How would that look if I did not provide food for my own family?" he asked her, bringing over a cup of coffee for himself. Unlike hers, which was a creamy color, his coffee was a deep, rich black.

"How would that look to whom?" Addie asked. The moment the words were out of her mouth, it occurred to her whom he might be thinking about. "Are you thinking about Zelda?" she asked him a little too innocently.

"I am thinking about my responsibility to you," he informed Addie. "Now, stop asking questions and eat while the food is still warm," Eduardo told his granddaughter.

Addie nodded. Maybe this was her grandfather's way of coping with the changes that were going on in his life. She was not about to argue with him. She wanted the man happy, so she focused on the food that Eduardo had set down in front of her.

Applying her fork to the egg, she brought the first warm piece up to her mouth. As she slipped the fork between her lips, the smile that rose in response was totally effortless.

She sighed happily. "You always did make the best sunny-side-up fried eggs in the world," she told her grandfather.

He didn't bother to argue the point. "That is thanks to your grandmother," he said with a warm, reminiscent smile. "That woman taught me everything that there was to know about how to cook."

"Wasn't that rather unusual back then?" Addie asked him as she continued eating. Her grandfather had never shared that fact with her before. Another sign, as far as she was concerned, that her grandfather was really trying to adjust to this new life that was facing him.

He smiled at Addie over his coffee cup. "Your grandmother liked to brag that I was a man who was ahead of my time."

Addie's eyes crinkled as she smiled back at the man she loved so dearly. "Ellie and I always felt that way."

"Now you are making me blush," Eduardo said with a dismissive wave of his hand. He set down his coffee cup. "Shall I pack a lunch for you?" he asked, rising as if she had already agreed.

Addie's first inclination was to turn down her grandfather's offer, falling back on the excuse she had already used, that she could always drop in at the diner if she was hungry.

But then she thought better of it and stopped herself. If it made her grandfather feel more useful to pack a lunch for her, who was she to turn down his offer?

So she said, "Thank you, Grandpa. That would be very nice." She flashed a wide smile at him, then continued eating her breakfast.

"Do you want me to use the baked ham I made the other day?" Eduardo offered.

Apparently, her grandfather had already thought this through, Addie mused. But, then, the man was always thorough.

"Yes, thank you," she told him, then repeated, "That would be very nice."

But rather than begin to make the sandwich for her, Eduardo turned around to face his granddaughter, scrutinizing her. "All right, Addie, why are you tiptoeing around me like this?" he asked.

"Tiptoeing," she repeated. And then she smiled as she nodded her head. "I have to admit, I'm impressed."

His eyes narrowed just a little. "You are also stalling," he pointed out. "Why?"

She didn't see any reason to try to lie to her grandfather. He usually saw through everything, anyway. "Because I know it's hard for you to adjust, having Ellie gone like this."

For a moment, Eduardo stared at Addie. And then he surprised her by laughing.

"Gone?" he repeated, as if it was some sort of a foreign word. "Your sister got married, Addie. She did not die. Besides, I still have you, the horses, the ranch hands and enough work to keep me very, very busy for a very long time. Now, finish eating your breakfast and go be part of building Forever its very first hospital."

Addie smiled up at the man. "I love you, Grandpa," she told him with feeling.

Eduardo nodded and beamed at her. "How could you not?" her grandfather asked. Spreading his hands, he told her, "I am very lovable."

Finished eating, she rose to her feet and gave him a kiss. "That you are," she said, "Grandpa. That you are." She took the wrapped sandwich from him and tucked it into her bag. "Try not to get into too much trouble while I'm gone."

He chuckled and gave her a knowing look. "I was going to say the same thing to you," he told his granddaughter.

* * *

Addie could feel the excitement all but crackling in the air as she drove into town. It was obvious that everyone knew things would be different once this project was finally off the ground and completed. When it was completed, Forever would be making a very progressive leap forward into the twenty-first century. After all, it wasn't every town that had a hospital, even a limited one.

Reaching her location, for the first time that she could remember, Addie found that parking her car was going to be a challenge. The contractor who was responsible for building Forever's first hotel had been included on this project, too, and she had brought in workers, all local, to frame the hospital now that the chosen land had been cleared and prepared.

Addie decided to park her car near the clinic, which had been reopened several years ago. It somehow seemed fitting.

She got out and made her way over toward the new hospital site that had once housed a rather large stable. In anticipation of the proposed project, more land had been purchased, some of which had been donated by residents who felt it was high time that civilization finally came to Forever.

Addie stood back for a few minutes, drinking it

all in, focusing on what the finished product would look like. And then she gradually became aware of all the activity.

Specifically, she focused on Jason.

He seemed to be at the very center of the activity, pointing in one direction, turning toward another, and all the while, directing the people who were surrounding him and telling them all what to do.

From the looks of it, the man had been at this for some time now and it was only a little after eight.

What time had he gotten started? she couldn't help wondering.

Moving in closer, she waited for a break in the activity before she tried to speak to him. But when there didn't seem as if there would be any, she decided to take her opportunity and placed a hand on Jason's arm.

His mind obviously elsewhere, Jason glanced at her. At first, it looked as if Addie's presence hardly registered. Determined, she tried to get his attention again. After all, he was in charge of the entire project.

"Adelyn Montenegro reporting for duty, Mr. Eastwood," she quipped brightly, waiting for the man to direct her.

Her salutation stopped Jason in his tracks. Nodding at the man he had just been talking to, he murmured, "That should keep you busy for now," and then he looked at Addie.

"You were serious about coming in to work on the hospital." There was a trace of surprise in his voice.

"I was," Addie answered, wondering why he would have thought otherwise.

Jason decided to plunge right in. "And what is it, exactly, that you can do on this project?" he asked.

As he recalled, their conversations on the topic of getting the hospital up and running hadn't exactly been all that clear and enlightening. He knew that, like everyone else, she thought that having a hospital in Forever was a good idea, but what, exactly, could she bring to the project?

"Whatever you need me to do," Addie answered. When she saw the way Jason's lips curved, she decided maybe it might be a good idea to explain that statement. "I can do anything with power tools, from the simple to the complex, that needs to be done. Whether it's creating hospital rooms for patients, areas to house laboratories or X-ray apparatus, or operating suites, I can do it. All I need are to see blueprints with the exact specifications and someone to point me in the right direction."

Jason nodded. She sounded confident enough,

but he'd come across people like that before—people who were clearly bluffing their way through a project. Those sorts of people could do a lot of damage if left on their own.

"And I take it that you can work well and play well with others." His expression was deadly serious as he said the mocking words.

"I thought I already proved that to you at the wedding," Addie deadpanned, her eyes never leaving his.

Jason inclined his head, vividly recalling every detail about the evening they had wound up spending together.

"That you did," he acknowledged. "All right, come with me," he said, leading her over toward a curtained-off area within the building-in-the-making. It was all clearly beginning to take shape, actually even faster than Jason had initially anticipated when he had come up with the design.

Just inside the curtain was a large folding table where the newly drawn-up blueprints were laid out. "Let me get you acquainted with my vision."

"Your vision?" she asked, following behind Jason to where the table was set up, trying not to mock him.

At first glance, it looked as if the table contained the complicated plans for the invasion of D-Day.

"Well, mine and Neil's," Jason clarified. He wanted to make sure that Neil got all the credit that was due him. After all, if his cousin hadn't suggested this project, he would have never gotten involved in the hospital's conception.

Jason looked over at her. He wasn't about to take anything for granted. "You do know how to read blueprints, right?"

She took a breath, searching for patience. Addie had thought that fact had already been established earlier.

"Are you planning on continuing to insult me, or are we going to get on with this?" she asked. "I could always take you back to the barn where Ellie houses her plane."

He eyed her quizzically. "Why would I want to see that again?" he asked. In his opinion, once was more than enough for him. And then the light suddenly dawned on him. "Did you...?"

She decided to spare him asking the rest of the question. "Once I realized that Ellie was serious about buying that old plane from the pilot, I knew she was going to need somewhere to house it, so I was the one who converted it from a barn into an airplane hangar," Addie told him.

Jason stared at her, torn between being stunned and impressed. "I thought everyone was just making it up," he admitted. "You actually *built* it?" he asked, as if he wasn't sure whether or not to believe what he was hearing. "Yourself?" She seemed awfully young to be in charge of something like that on her own.

"I *converted* it," Addie corrected. "Grandpa built the original barn, but I was the one who made it into an airplane hangar. Any other questions?"

He looked at her. A ton of questions flooded his mind, but for now, he decided to let them go unspoken. "Not at the moment." He smiled, thinking that he should be prepared for anything, and said, "All right, since you're serious, let's get to work."

Addie nodded. "Fine with me," she responded. She was more than eager to leave her mark on Forever's new hospital…and maybe, just maybe, to gain Jason's respect.

Chapter Eight

Jason felt as if he had been working nonstop since a little before six thirty in the morning. By late afternoon, he was more than a little drained. When the clock finally struck 6:30 p.m., an eternity later, he would have loved to have called it a day. But he wasn't about to ask anything of the people working under him that he wasn't asking of himself.

Certainly not when this project was getting off the ground so well.

Oh, the actual building had already been put in place, transported piecemeal and put together so that only an expert would have been able to see that it hadn't been built right there from scratch.

But there was still a great deal left to do before the hospital was anywhere near finished. And that didn't begin to account for transforming the building's interior so that it could be called an actual functioning hospital.

Like all the other projects he had been involved in, completion came about one step at a time, although Jason was determined to push for giant steps.

So far, he thought, so good.

As for Addie, she had been working steadily since Jason had shown her the blueprints and told her what he wanted to be addressed first. Since she hadn't heard anything from him in hours, by the time six thirty rolled around, she went looking for him in order to check on the builder.

As near as she could tell, Jason had been working just as steadily as she had. Possibly, she estimated, even more so. There had been none of this attitude of "I'm the supervisor, you're the lackey" coming from the man. Jason, she was happy to see, worked every bit as hard as the people he was employing.

He also seemed to have more energy than anyone. Considering what this hospital meant to everyone, that was almost hard to believe. Yet he seemed to be almost everywhere, going nonstop.

"Something wrong?" Jason asked when he finally realized that she had been standing there, observing him, for what might have been quite a while now.

"No," Addie answered. "I just came to see if maybe you were ready to call it a day, or at the very least, get something to eat to refuel."

Jason looked at her, slightly disoriented. "Why?" he asked, putting aside his blueprints. "What time is it?"

She realized that he was serious. He had apparently lost track of time.

"You really do get wrapped up in your work, don't you? It's late," she told him. "I thought we might stop by Miss Joan's to get some dinner."

"We?" he asked as if she had abruptly just slipped into a foreign language he couldn't quite grasp.

As far as she could tell, she hadn't said anything all that confusing. Why was he acting as if he was having trouble following her?

"Unless you've already made arrangements to eat with someone else," she qualified.

"No," he said, placing his blueprints into the large leather binder he had opened on the table.

After closing it, he tied the two sides of the binder together. "It's not that. I'm just surprised that you wouldn't be going home to have dinner with your grandfather."

She thought about her conversation with her grandfather that morning and how badly she'd felt for him when she had assumed that he was suffering from partial empty-nest syndrome. But he had gone on to lay out such a busy agenda, she thought that maybe she was interfering in the man's life by popping up too early.

He had acted so proud of her for being part of the crew building the hospital. Maybe having her working with Neil's cousin was somehow good for her grandfather's mental state. Besides, it felt good to be bringing in money. The ranch could certainly use some things.

"My grandfather's busy," she told him simply. "And besides, I'll see him tonight when I finally get in. You, however, don't really know that many people in Forever yet, so I thought perhaps you might like some company when you get something to eat, especially seeing as how we're family now and all."

For some odd reason, the phrase "kissing cousins" flashed through Jason's mind. He found himself wondering just how that would feel.

The very next second, he banished the idea from his mind. This was definitely not the time to explore that thought.

Instead, he told her, "I'd like that. Just let me wind up a few things first."

"You're the boss, Jason," Addie said as she gestured toward the structure he had just emerged out of.

He smiled at her, thinking that had a nice ring to it. The problem was, he wasn't sure just how serious she really was, applying that phrase to him.

He figured he'd find out eventually.

"We'll go in separate vehicles," she told Jason when he finally returned some fifteen minutes later.

"You're going to have to be seen with me when we're eating at the diner, or are you thinking separate tables, too?" he asked.

"It has nothing to do with being seen with you." The man really had a way of misunderstanding things, she thought. "After we finish eating, we'll each be going our separate ways. I'll be going back to the ranch and you'll be going back to Neil's house…unless you're going to be going back to work on the hospital for some reason."

The separate-cars comment made sense now.

Jason laughed at himself, then shook his head. He was more tired than he'd thought.

"I'm devoted to my work," he readily told Addie. "But I'm not a fanatic about it. I think putting in a fourteen hour day is pretty much my limit."

"You actually started that early?" Addie asked, surprised. She knew Jason had come in to work ahead of her, but she hadn't thought he'd gotten in *that* early.

Jason shrugged in response. "I had these ideas I wanted to get started on," he told her. And then he saw the way she was smiling. The woman really did have a very captivating smile. Was it at his expense? "What?" he asked as they walked back to where their cars were parked.

Jason noted belatedly that most of the other vehicles had cleared out already.

"Looks like Forever's certainly getting its money's worth," she observed. The parking lot had really been full earlier, fuller than she ever remembered seeing it. She hadn't realized just how many people were employed on this project. "Follow me to Miss Joan's."

"Why, do you think I'll get lost?" he asked. In comparison to some of the places he'd worked, this town was the size of a quarter.

"No, but I think you might change your mind

and decide to skip Miss Joan's and go raid Neil's refrigerator instead."

He grinned, almost sheepishly. "Can't. I did that yesterday," he confessed. "There's not all that much left in the refrigerator to raid. Remind me to restock it before the happy groom comes back from his honeymoon. It won't do to start out a marriage with an empty refrigerator."

Her mouth curved. The man was really human after all, she thought.

"Good thinking," Addie told him, opening the driver's-side door and getting into her vehicle.

Putting the key into the ignition, she waited until Jason got in behind the wheel of his car. Then she started up her vehicle.

It wasn't that far to Miss Joan's diner.

As usual, the parking lot that surrounded the diner was full. Addie waited until Jason pulled up two spots next to hers and then got out.

She saw the way he was looking at the diner's lot.

"Is it always this full?" he asked. He'd thought that maybe Miss Joan has just exaggerated the situation the last time. Didn't any of these people ever eat at home? he wondered.

"The food's good and people like the camaraderie," Addie replied. "So, more or less to some degree, yes."

As he approached the diner, he looked at it thoughtfully. "You know, Miss Joan's diner might not be a bad place for an investment," he observed.

"Unless you think that making an investment entitles you to have some say in how the business is run," Addie told him in all seriousness. "Because it really doesn't," she assured Jason. "Miss Joan has the first—and last— word when it comes to running that diner. She has *never* liked having anyone tell her what to do."

He had already gotten the impression that the woman was headstrong, but he thought that she and her husband were equal partners in the diner. "Not even her husband?"

Addie climbed up the stairs. "Miss Joan makes some allowances for him," she said. "But Harry wouldn't have survived this long with Miss Joan if the man didn't know when to hold his tongue."

She saw the judgmental look that came over Jason's face. She didn't want him thinking negative things about Miss Joan and hurried to rectify that impression.

"As irritating as Miss Joan might appear when you first meet her, she does have a great many good qualities about her. She just doesn't advertise them...and Harry does love her dearly."

Jason nodded, taking Addie at her word, although he really wasn't all that convinced himself.

"If you say so," Jason said, pushing open the diner's front door and holding it for Addie.

"You'll learn," was all Addie said as she walked into the diner.

Despite the fact that she was busy with a customer, Miss Joan looked toward the front door immediately. Her expression never changed as she asked the duo, "So how did your very first day on the job go?"

The question, coming from the rear of the diner, caught Jason entirely off guard. "That woman has ears like a bat, doesn't she?" he asked Addie.

"'That woman' also knows how to read lips, Builder Boy, and her eyesight's as good as an army marksman's," Miss Joan informed Jason as they came closer. She gestured toward the counter. There were exactly two empty seats there, located side by side. "Sit down and take a load off." Her eyes pinned Jason. "I hear you've been working all day."

Jason looked at Addie, amazed. "Is there anything that woman doesn't know?" he asked, freshly stunned.

Addie merely smiled at Jason's display of innocence.

"You're beginning to learn," she told him. She decided to leave the choice of seating up to him. He needed to retain some dignity. "Counter or table?"

He glanced thoughtfully toward Miss Joan. "She'll probably be able to hear us no matter where we sit. You choose."

Looking over her shoulder, Addie was about to pick the only empty table available when she saw that her grandfather was sitting at a table in the back with Miss Joan's sister. From the way they were looking at one another, they didn't seem to be aware of anyone else in the premises except for each other.

Deciding to give her grandfather and the woman their privacy, Addie suggested, "Why don't we just sit at the counter? That way there won't be any question in your mind that Miss Joan can hear us and it isn't just hocus-pocus on her part," she told Jason.

"I'm already more than half convinced that the woman is a witch. The only question that remains is…is her sister?" He watched the look of surprise pass over Addie's face and answered her unspoken question. "Yes, I saw Zelda sitting with your grandfather."

Addie put her own interpretation to Jason's previous question.

"The only danger my grandfather is in is getting caught in the crossfire that might wind up erupting between Miss Joan and her sister," Addie told him in a low voice. She fervently hoped that the din coming from within the diner might wind up covering their conversation.

"I thought that Miss Joan and Zelda had declared a truce and that everything that had happened years earlier had been forgiven," Jason said. "Or did I get that wrong?"

"You didn't get that wrong," Addie told him. "It's just that sometimes, Miss Joan has trouble remembering that she was the one who had actually instituted the truce. It seems that some of the old wounds between them pop up and bleed every now and then," she admitted.

It wasn't as if this was something new. Jason had certainly seen his share of arguments and differences between people in the various places he had worked.

"I guess small towns and big cities all have the same problem," he said.

Addie nodded in agreement. "At bottom, people

are just people. Some are kinder, some are not, but they're really not all that different."

Miss Joan chose that moment to pop up between them out of the blue. "I suppose you saw my sister cozying up to your grandfather," the woman said as she presented each of them with a menu. When Addie didn't say anything, Miss Joan made her an offer. "If you like, I can go up and tell Zelda that she's needed in the back."

That didn't sound very fair. "Is she working today?" Addie asked. She hadn't gotten that impression, but she could have been wrong.

Miss Joan waved her hand. "Doesn't matter. When you work at the diner, you can always be pressed into service if the need comes up. All my people know that."

Miss Joan began to move around the counter, about to go to the rear of the diner, but Addie put her hand on the woman's wrist to hold her in place.

"That's all right, Miss Joan," she told her. "My grandfather could use the company."

"Not that kind of company," Miss Joan told her. "If you ask me, your grandfather deserves better."

Addie's eyes met Miss Joan's. "You're being kind of hard on her, aren't you?" she asked the diner owner.

"Sometimes I don't think I'm being hard enough," Miss Joan replied. "The offer still stands."

When Addie let the matter go, Miss Joan switched gears. "So what can I get you two?" she asked. "Angel has only a few orders of chicken pot pie left. I would suggest getting one while you can." Her hazel eyes washed over the pair, coming to rest on Jason.

He felt that if he turned down Miss Joan's offer, that would somehow be perceived as an insult by the woman. So he didn't.

"I'll take an order," Jason told her.

"You'll split an order," Miss Joan informed him decisively, nodding toward Addie. "Otherwise you won't be able to walk out of here. Angel is very generous with her ingredients. By the way," she went on before she turned to give her chef the order, "how's our new hospital coming along?"

"It's too soon to call it a new hospital," Jason answered. "Right now, it's still a hospital-in-progress."

Miss Joan frowned. "I didn't ask for an argument about terminology. Is it coming along or not?"

"So far, there are no major problems," he told her.

"Doesn't like to commit himself, does he?" Miss Joan asked, looking at Addie.

Addie smiled as she nodded. "That way, no one can call him on it."

"Cagey," Miss Joan pronounced. "I'd watch myself around this one," she warned Addie just before she walked away from them.

That, Addie thought, had already been duly noted.

Chapter Nine

Jason frowned slightly as he watched Miss Joan make her way behind the counter, moving toward the kitchen. "That woman has a personality like a persimmon," he muttered.

"She'll grow on you," Addie told him, not for the first time.

"You mean like fungus?" Jason asked with a touch of sarcasm, thinking he could easily see the similarity.

"No, like the decent woman that she is," Addie told him, growing just a touch defensive. "She was there for Ellie and me when we suddenly found ourselves orphaned."

"I thought you said your grandfather raised you."

"He did," she confirmed. "But first he had to get here…after identifying my parents." Her expression grew very serious. "My parents and grandmother—Grandpa's wife—were killed in a car accident. They were checking out a location for their very first vacation since they had gotten married." Addie took a deep breath, separating herself from the sad memories that story created. "Miss Joan took care of us while my grandfather tended to all the details, including making all three identifications.

"Because of circumstances," Addie continued, "my grandfather couldn't pay for the funeral. Miss Joan was the one who took care of all that. *And* she refused to let him pay her back. She told him that he had enough on his shoulders to deal with." Addie finally turned to look at Jason. "That's the kind of person she is. Now do you understand why I feel about her the way I do?"

"I'm beginning to," Jason replied.

Just then, Miss Joan returned with a large chicken pot pie and set the pie tin on the counter between the duo. Raising her eyes, the woman was about to say something about the meal. But then she stopped, noting the way that Jason was looking at her.

Her question was directed at Addie. "Why is Builder Boy looking at me like he had just heard rumors that I was some mythical fairy godmother he was expecting to appear?"

Addie raised her shoulders in a mystified shrug. "I have no idea, Miss Joan," she replied innocently. "Maybe he's heard stories about your good deeds."

Miss Joan shot her a penetrating look. "And maybe someone's been running off at the mouth when she shouldn't have."

Addie continued to be the soul of innocence. "I guess we'll never know, will we?"

Miss Joan laughed harshly. "You're making me rethink what I was about to suggest."

Jason decided it was about time that he participated in this little dialogue before the older woman thought of him as being totally spineless.

"And what was it that you were about to suggest?" he asked.

"How about that? He *can* talk," Miss Joan marveled. "I was going to suggest that we all gather next Saturday to officially welcome Builder Boy here—" she waved her hand at Jason "—to Forever and show him our gratitude for his finally turning the hospital we've been patiently waiting for into an honest-to-goodness reality."

Although the words were close to flattering, he felt that they weren't really true yet, which meant that he couldn't take any real credit for them.

"The completed project isn't going to be a reality for a long while," Jason pointed out.

"Humph," Miss Joan said, making a dismissive noise. "That first nail that you hammered in was a step closer to making the hospital a reality," she told him.

Jason opened his mouth to contradict Miss Joan again, but got no closer to uttering it than parting his lips.

Addie held her hand up and put it against his mouth to hold back any words he might have to say on the subject.

"Just agree with her, Jason. Trust me, it's really a lot smarter and simpler that way," she told him.

"I'd listen to her if I were you," Miss Joan said "She's a really bright girl. I taught her everything she ever needed to know," she added with pride. And then she waved one gnarled hand toward the pie that was still sitting on the counter between their two plates. "Now I'd eat that pot pie before it begins to harden and you wind up hurting Angel's feelings."

Miss Joan gave Jason a very pointed look before she turned her attention to one of her other customers.

A moment later, Jason realized something. "I never gave her my answer about that party idea she just proposed."

"Yeah, you did," Addie told him, grinning. "You said yes."

He looked at her, totally perplexed. To the best of his knowledge, he hadn't said a word in response.

"When?" he asked.

The man had a lot to learn about Miss Joan, Addie thought. "When you didn't immediately tell her 'hell no.' Don't feel bad," she said, guessing his reaction. "Nobody says no to Miss Joan."

"Well," he said thoughtfully, "you did say that she took you and your sister in while waiting for your grandfather to come and take over raising you. That means that there has to be some good in the woman, right?"

"Absolutely," Addie agreed with feeling.

Jason decided he needed to change the subject. It was safer that way. Looking down at his plate, he said, "This chicken pot pie is really good. Do you know if it's going to be served at the party?"

Menus hadn't been discussed, but Addie was

certain that Angel would be in charge of the food. She knew from experience that Angel was always amenable to suggestions, especially when those suggestions involved the guest of honor.

"I don't see why not," Addie said to Neil's cousin.

"Good," Jason nodded. This had to be the best chicken pot pie he had ever eaten, bar none, and he had sampled a variety of food from all around the country. "Then I'll definitely come."

It wasn't easy, but Addie managed to suppress the grin that was struggling to emerge.

"I'm sure Miss Joan will appreciate that," Addie replied.

"Good, I wouldn't want to do anything that would wind up offending the woman," Jason told Addie.

Addie finally wound up losing her struggle with the grin fighting to materialize.

Jason felt as if he had missed the punch line on some inside joke. "What?"

"I'm afraid that boat has already sailed," Addie told him. "Lucky for you, Miss Joan is a great believer in second chances."

"I think Miss Joan's sister might have another opinion about that," he said.

Miss Joan might believe in second chances,

but third chances were another story. "You keep thinking that way and you might not see the inside of that welcome-to-Forever party after all," Addie said.

Pausing, she debated for a moment. She knew she might regret saying this, but she forged ahead, anyway. "Look, this is between Miss Joan and Zelda. However they wind up resolving this is up to them. I think everyone else should just stay out of it."

"How about you?" Jason challenged. "Are you going to stay out of it?"

"Of course."

There was that innocence again. Jason eyed her doubtfully. "Even though your grandfather is involved in this matter?" he asked pointedly.

"Especially since my grandfather is involved," she answered. Then, after a beat, she added, "At least for now."

Jason nodded, a knowing look slipping over his face. "I thought so."

It was exactly at this point that Miss Joan chose to return to where they were both seated at the counter.

"So how's everything?" she asked, her sweeping gaze taking in the duo and the counter before them. The expression on the older woman's face bore testimony to the fact that she didn't expect to be on the receiving end of any complaints.

"The food is spectacular," Jason freely told the woman.

Miss Joan nodded, as if his answer didn't surprise her. "And the other thing we discussed?"

For a moment, Jason looked as if Miss Joan had lost him. Miss Joan, in turn, looked at Addie. "The boy doesn't have much of an attention span, does he?" Shaking her head, Miss Joan's eyes returned to Jason. "The welcome-to-Forever party?" the woman pressed.

Before he could answer, Addie decided to come to the builder's rescue. "You have to understand, Miss Joan. Jason has a great deal on his mind. And don't forget, this was his very first day on the job. Jason still has a lot of strings to pull, a lot of pieces to get moving on the chessboard," Addie explained.

Miss Joan's expression grew thoughtful, as if she was trying to make up her mind about something.

"Is she always going to do the talking for you?" she finally asked, her eyes pinning Jason in his seat.

Jason suddenly felt as if he was eighteen again, catapulted back to his early college days and being grilled by a tough professor.

"Only if she's telling you exactly what I intended to tell you," he told the woman in an easy manner.

For a moment, Miss Joan's face didn't register anything at all, and then, ever so slowly, the smallest of smiles blossomed on the woman's lips. "Good to know. So then you'll be here on Saturday," she said confidently. It was no longer a question. "The party starts at noon," she went on to tell him. Then, in case he was wondering why a party for adults was starting so early, Miss Joan explained, "It's so that parents with little ones are able to come to it as well without having to deal with cranky kids. Kids get cranky if they stay up too late."

Hazel eyes swept over the empty pie tin and the plates that had all but been wiped completely clean. Satisfaction rose in Miss Joan's eyes. "Anything else I can get you?"

Jason shook his head. "Just the check," he answered.

But Miss Joan made no effort to comply. "Sorry," she told the builder. "No can do."

Again the woman had managed to lose him. Was there some sort of protocol to follow before a check for a meal could be issued? "And why's that?" he asked.

"Because dinner was on the house," Miss Joan told the builder.

In Jason's experience, accepting a meal "on the house" just put him in someone's debt. He frowned.

"I don't like being in anyone's debt," Jason readily informed the woman.

Miss Joan raised her chin. "And I happen to like getting my way. Calm down, Builder Boy. I wasn't trying to trade dinner for your soul." There was just the tiniest bit of admiration in her hazel eyes, which were now sweeping over him. "I didn't know you people from back East had so much integrity."

"Well, we do," he answered, getting off the stool, then waiting for Addie to join him. "So can I have the check?" he asked, assuming this was now a done deal.

"No," Miss Joan answered as she turned on her heel and walked away.

Jason stared after the woman, an incredulous expression on his face. "I thought the argument was settled," he said, completely caught off guard.

"It was," Addie easily answered. "Just not the way that you had expected it to be." She smiled at him. "Take a piece of advice. The round belongs to Miss Joan. Most of the rounds belong to Miss

Joan. The sooner you make peace with that, the easier your life around here is going to be."

Jason sighed, shaking his head and murmuring something under his breath she couldn't readily make out.

He followed Addie to the front door. "You really believe that?"

"With every fiber of my being," Addie answered with a wide smile.

On her way out, she glanced toward where her grandfather and Zelda had been sitting. That table now had another couple sitting there. When had Zelda and her grandfather left? Addie wondered. She certainly hadn't noticed them leaving.

For now, she didn't say anything.

As she and Jason walked out of the diner, Addie looked at him. "Do you feel drained?"

He laughed dryly. "I felt drained when I came in," he replied.

The man was avoiding the question, Addie thought. She was beginning to expect that. Determined to pin him down, she pressed, "But more so now?"

Jason shrugged, then murmured, "I guess. This is a new project, and as such, it takes some getting used to. They all do," he added philosophically. This was nothing new for him.

"That's not because it's a new project," Addie explained. "That's because Miss Joan takes more than a little getting used to. There's no shame in admitting that," Addie told him as she slid into her car seat.

She closed her door, then rolled down her window and looked up, pinning Jason in place as she stressed, "Remember that."

He frowned, dismissing her remark. "Uh-huh." He hardly sounded convinced.

"By the way…" she added pointedly through her opened window.

Jason looked at her, waiting to hear some off-hand, possibly irritating parting remark from her. "Yes?"

"You did good," Addie told him with a wide smile.

Was she just trying to placate him or stroke his ego? Or was he being set up? He found that he hadn't learned what to make of any given situation. Working with his hands proved to be a great deal simpler.

"How can you tell?" Jason challenged, still not a hundred percent sure what Addie was referring to.

"Miss Joan was smiling as she walked away," Addie said, clearing up at least part of the mystery.

She was talking about his last encounter with the diner owner, not anything else.

She added, "That doesn't happen as often as you might think," then pulled out of the parking lot and drove away, leaving Jason staring after her.

Chapter Ten

When Addie pulled up in front of her ranch house half an hour later, she was surprised to see her grandfather's truck parked right out in front. She parked her vehicle right next to it, then got out and closed the door.

"Well, this is interesting," she murmured. Thinking that the man might have been entertaining, she entered the house very quietly. As she closed the door behind her, Addie called out, "I'm home, Grandpa," just in case she was inadvertently interrupting something between her grandfather and Zelda.

But Eduardo was in the living room and apparently alone. Seeing Addie, he smiled at her.

"So how was your first day on the job?" he asked.

She let out a long breath, then answered, "Exhausting." Addie paused by the sofa. All she wanted to do was go to bed, but she couldn't just ignore her grandfather, especially when there were questions crowding her head. "Why didn't you come by to say hello?" she asked as she sat down beside him.

"I didn't want to interrupt you while you were working," he answered.

"No, I'm talking about at Miss Joan's diner. Why didn't you come by and say something then?"

When Eduardo continued looking at her with the same innocent expression, Addie raised her eyebrows. "Don't give me that look, Grandpa. I saw you sitting in the back of the diner with Zelda."

"We just came in to get some coffee," her grandfather told her. "You and Jason were talking to Miss Joan. I didn't want to interrupt you."

Addie stared down the man she had always held in such very high esteem. Was he afraid of what she might think about his being with Zelda? Or had Miss Joan's opinion about her grandfather spending time with Zelda managed to color everything? In either case, she wanted him to know that she and her sister were completely on-board with whatever was going on.

Addie took the older man's hand and held it in both of hers. "Grandpa, Ellie and I think that you seeing Zelda is wonderful. We're both *very* happy that you've found someone to spend some time with. Actually, Grandpa, it's about time," she insisted. "You've spent many too many years devoting yourself exclusively to us."

Eduardo shrugged his shoulders. It was obvious that the man wasn't comfortable with the subject. "I feel guilty about all of this."

Addie's eyebrows drew together. "You don't feel guilty because of us, do you, Grandpa?" she asked. "Because you have to realize that you shouldn't."

Eduardo sighed, searching for the right words. Finally, when they continued to elude him, he just blurted out the truth.

"I feel guilty because of your grandmother."

Addie's heart really went out to him. "Grandpa, everything you have ever told me about Grandma points to the fact that she was a very wonderful, kindhearted woman—" she began.

"Oh, that she was," Eduardo said with feeling. "She really was."

"Then, if you ask me," Addie continued, "my guess is that Grandma would be cheering you on." She looked into the man's sad eyes. "She wouldn't want you to spend the rest of your life all alone."

"But I'm not alone," Eduardo told her warmly. "I have you girls."

"And you always will," Addie informed him. "But Ellie's married now and maybe someday, who knows, I will be, too. In any case, you don't need to feel as if you have to hover over us constantly and, more importantly, you need to have a life of your own, too."

Eduardo looked as if he was torn between what she was saying and the way he felt. "Miss Joan—" he began, about to protest, but she interrupted him.

"Miss Joan has a husband," Addie gently pointed out to her grandfather. Everyone in town really liked Harry Monroe and had been in his corner even before he ever proposed to Miss Joan. "A very sweet man who will remind her that she forgave Zelda for what happened years ago and that she had promised that she was determined to move forward."

Eduardo pressed his lips together and nodded. "You're right."

"Of course, I'm right," Addie insisted, as if there was no question about that. "And you are also the one who taught Ellie and me all about the difference between right and wrong. If Miss Joan gives you and Zelda a hard time about being together, you just let me know and I'll handle it."

Eduardo's mouth curved in amusement. "You will handle it," he repeated.

"That's what I said. Nobody is going to interfere with my grandpa finding the true happiness that he deserves," Addie told him with feeling.

Eduardo laughed, his eyes shining, and he kissed the top of her head. "You are a good girl, Addie."

"Anything I am it's thanks to you. Now," she said, rising to her feet, "if you don't mind, I am going to drag myself up to bed. It has been a very long, long day."

Eduardo nodded and waved her up the stairs. "I will see you in the morning."

"Right," she murmured.

Barely aware of doing it, Addie put one foot in front of the other. With effort, she forced herself to focus on getting up the staircase and to her room.

Addie didn't even bother changing out of her clothes. The last thing she actually remembered was landing facedown in her bed.

She was sound asleep before she had even made contact with her pillow.

* * *

Addie woke up with a start the following morning. It took her a moment to realize that she had slept like a dead person for eight hours. Moving quickly, she showered, got dressed and then came flying downstairs.

When she did, Addie found her breakfast waiting for her on the table and a packed lunch right beside it. It was a replay of the day before.

Almost.

The only component that appeared to be missing was her grandfather. He was nowhere to be found in the house. Addie decided that he was probably trying to get a jump on his day, as well.

Either that, or he was trying to squeeze in some alone time with Zelda before she was supposed to be at work. But if that was the case, it was her grandfather's business and she needed to stop butting in.

Addie's mouth curved. Easier said than done, she thought, moving back to the kitchen table. No matter how well intentioned her thoughts were about boundaries and keeping them, her small family was her first priority.

She needed to be certain that everything was all right with her grandfather and this new person who seemed so important in his life. Ellie's life was all in order and she appeared to be very happy. Addie wanted to make sure that her grandfather's life was that way, too.

And, if they were happy, then *she* was happy. It was as simple as that.

She finished eating her breakfast quickly. After washing and putting away the dishes, Addie then picked up the lunch her grandfather had packed for her. As she left the house, she noted that his truck was missing. That meant that he had either gotten a really early start on the day…or he had gone to see Zelda.

Either way, he was doing something that he enjoyed. And that was all that really mattered, she silently insisted.

As she drove toward town, Addie remembered that she hadn't said anything to her grandfather about the party that Miss Joan was throwing for Jason at the diner this Saturday. She felt guilty about the omission even though, more than likely, word of mouth would bring the news to her grandfather before she could.

Addie thought about the proposed party. She hoped that her grandfather would bring Zelda with him and that Miss Joan wouldn't say anything to change that, or make them uncomfortable.

Recalling the way Eduardo and Zelda had been

looking at one another last night, for all intents and purposes, they were already a couple. They just needed to admit it to each other…and to keep Miss Joan from throwing obstacles in their path.

When Addie arrived at the hospital site, she parked her vehicle and went inside, and found that Jason was already there. And, like her, he was getting a head start on the day.

She wasn't surprised.

They obviously had the same work ethic. The idea warmed her, but she didn't explore it any further. But she did really hope that Jason found the fact that they had something in common equally comforting when he became aware of it.

Addie initially debated whether or not to announce her presence when she walked in, but she found that she didn't have to. Jason looked up from what he was doing before she had gotten halfway across the area, on her way past his work desk.

Laying aside his pen, Jason rose. Addie had come in early yesterday, but this was day two and first impressions were now a thing of the past as far as he was concerned. That meant that this might be the way she always operated.

"So, you always make a habit of coming in

early?" he asked her point-blank, as if they were already in the middle of a conversation.

The last thing she wanted Jason to think was that she was doing this to impress him. "I find it's easier getting started before there are too many distractions around," she answered.

Jason nodded as he took her words in. "Good work ethic," he said.

"I'm glad you approve."

Jason couldn't tell if she was being serious or sarcastic. Her expression was difficult to read, so he decided to put himself in her place.

"I didn't mean to sound condescending," he said.

At that point, Addie smiled at him. "It's something you can work on," she said lightly.

"Maybe you can give me pointers," Jason countered.

The man was still being somewhat sarcastic, she thought. Addie decided to play along. "Maybe," she agreed.

Jason held up a yellow pad. From the looks of it, the ink was still fresh. Apparently he wasn't devoted to his tablet the way so many people were these days. They had that in common, too, she thought. There was a great deal of writing on the yellow pad.

"Is that my to-do list?" she asked.

He didn't answer her question directly. "I've got a list of things that need to be attended to."

She took the pad from him, looking it over. Her mouth curved. "And here I thought I was just going to be watching my nail polish dry."

"Not today," he informed her in the same tone she had just used.

The list he had just handed her contained many varied tasks. "Anything on this list you want addressed first?" she asked. It didn't seem to be in any particular order.

"I'll leave that to your discretion," Jason told her.

She looked at the list again, slower this time. It still didn't seem to be in any particular order of importance. "You must have some preference in what you want done first."

"Yes," he admitted. His eyes met hers. "Everything."

All right, she'd play along, she thought.

Addie folded the list and tucked it into her back pocket.

"I'll see what I can do. Oh, and by the way, I brought you breakfast," Addie told him, handing Jason the bag that contained her lunch. She didn't think her grandfather would mind very much, seeing as how this was the man who was in charge of building the hospital. She could always pick up something at the diner later if she felt hungry.

"You didn't think that I could make my own breakfast?" he asked her, partially amused.

"Oh, I'm sure you can," she told him, not wanting to offend him. "But you did say that there was nothing left in Neil's refrigerator. You asked me to remind you to restock it and since I didn't…" She shrugged her shoulders by way of a further explanation.

Jason nodded. "Point taken," he acknowledged, giving up any pretense that he felt she had jumped the gun by preparing something for him to eat. He really wasn't all that good a cook, anyway.

Opening the bag, he looked in. The tempting smell of ham instantly wafted up to meet him. "Smells good."

"I know. I wasn't planning on poisoning you until after you finish the hospital," she said cheerfully.

He stared at her for a long moment, then realized she was kidding. At times he found it hard to tell. "Okay, I'll work slow," he told her, since supposedly she wouldn't "poison" him until he finished this project.

"Slow is always better," she agreed. "As long as it also includes being thorough."

Jason held up the bag she had just given him. "Thanks for this."

"Don't mention it," she replied, then pulled out the list he had handed her and got to work.

The rest of that morning went more or less the same way that the first one had. It was filled from one end to the other with details.

There was more equipment to track down and order, as well as finding a number of X-ray machines and apparatus that had been discussed yesterday.

All this was done against a background of noise created by things being retrofitted, nailed and renovated.

"You know," Addie murmured to herself later that day as she sat poring over the list, "I had no idea that there were so many things that went into making up a hospital."

"You'd be surprised just how much goes into building a functioning hospital," Jason said as he walked into the area where she was working. "From every single one of the nails that are driven into the walls to the paper needed to print out and compare the specs on all the required laboratory statistics."

Addie jumped and swung around to face the builder, her hand pressed against her pounding chest. She had really thought she was here by herself.

"Do you enjoy sneaking up on people?" she asked sharply.

Jason inclined his head, a hint of a smile playing on his lips. "Some more than others," he answered. "But, for the record, I'm sorry if I startled you. That wasn't my intent."

"And what *was* your intent?" Addie asked, trying to hide her reaction behind her indignation.

"Just to get a few answers," Jason said honestly.

Her eyes narrowed. "When I have some, I'll give them to you," she told the builder. "Right now, I'm just reviewing—for a second time—the list that you handed me. That is one *extremely* long list."

"There's a reason for that," Jason told her.

"And that is?" Addie asked, guessing that he was going to give her some flimsy excuse that wouldn't hold water. She still felt that he was trying to test her mettle.

"I always found it a good idea to press the most capable person into service. In this case, that person is you…unless you would rather just step away from that honor."

She gazed at him, half expecting that he was going to tell her that he was just kidding, or pulling her leg.

But he didn't.

She was being too sensitive. That normally didn't happen. "Sorry, I guess I'm just being a little too suspicious."

"Suspicion has its place," he acknowledged. "As long as it can, in the long run, help you to get your job successfully done. You'd be surprised how often things get done because the worker who is tasked with doing whatever is required is suspicious and puts that to its best use."

Addie laughed under her breath as she shook her head. "You make building sound like it's some sort of murder mystery."

"There are similarities that can be found between what you're doing and an unfolding mystery," Jason told her.

"Yes," Addie replied, looking up into Jason's eyes. "I think I definitely would be surprised," she agreed.

It took him a second to stop looking into her eyes and tear himself away. "Well, I'd better be getting back to work," Jason told her. "See you later."

"Later," she murmured.

That man had the most incredible eyes, she thought as she watched him walk away.

Chapter Eleven

It had become Eduardo's newly acquired habit to stop in town several times a week and, while there, swing by Miss Joan's. He told himself that it was so he could have a freshly made cup of rich coffee and a piece of sumptuous pie before turning his attention to whatever he had to do on the ranch that day.

Never mind that there would have been a lot less traveling involved if he had just had a pie waiting for him in the refrigerator and poured himself a cup of coffee from the pot he always brewed first thing in the morning.

It wasn't the pie or the coffee that spoke to him—it was being able to see Zelda that actually drew him to the diner.

And Eduardo's increased trips to the diner didn't go unnoticed.

Miss Joan decided that enough was enough. Having made up her mind, Miss Joan was quick to act and spoke to her sister first thing in the morning.

"Zelda, I'd like a word, please," Miss Joan said to her sister in her most authoritative voice. The diner was just about to open to admit its first early morning customers.

Zelda crossed the floor, approaching her sister apprehensively. She knew that stern voice well. "Is there something you need me to do?" Zelda asked.

"Yes," Miss Joan answered, giving her sister a pointed look. Memories from the past, no matter how much she was attempting to block them, kept insisting on raising their heads. "I need you to stay away from Eduardo Montenegro."

There was no arguing with the woman's tone.

Zelda tried, anyway. "But I'm not bothering him," she protested, then pointed out, "Eduardo asks for me."

"And that is bothering me," Miss Joan said with emphasis. "That man has had to deal with quite a lot. His wife died in the same car accident that killed his son and daughter-in-law. Eduardo has had to raise those two little granddaughters on his own for most of their lives. The man doesn't need any more complications in his life." Her hazel eyes narrowed. "Do I make myself clear?" Miss Joan demanded.

"I'm not trying to complicate it," Zelda protested.

Zelda wasn't trying to argue with her sister. Ever since she had come back into Miss Joan's life, Zelda had been desperately trying to make up for the wrong that she had done to her sister. Recently, it seemed as if everything was finally— *finally*—back on track. But ever since Eduardo had begun to pay attention to her, her sister had gone back to being irritable and highly critical, finding fault in absolutely everything she did.

"Just having you there, hovering around him like an insatiable mosquito in the summertime, complicates it." Miss Joan's hazel eyes all but bore holes in Zelda. "Now leave the man alone. Do I make myself clear?"

For a moment, Zelda contemplated talking back to her sister, but then she pressed her lips together. Taking a long breath, she backed down.

"All right," Zelda reluctantly agreed. "I will."

Harry had walked into the diner at the tail end of the exchange, or rather his wife's part of it. There was no real need to hear the whole thing. It wasn't all that hard for Harry to be able to fill in the blanks.

He waited until Zelda left the dining area before approaching his wife.

Sensing his presence, Miss Joan turned around quickly. Her thin, penciled-in eyebrows drew together. "I know that look, Harry."

"What look, Joannie?" he asked his wife innocently.

"The look that says I shouldn't have said what I said to Zelda. And don't call me 'Joannie,'" she told him sharply. "You know how I hate being called that."

Harry inclined his head. There were times when she didn't mind hearing him call her by the endearing nickname. "Sorry."

Miss Joan huffed. "Besides, you should be on my side. I was just trying to protect Eduardo. You know what Zelda's like."

"No, I remember what Zelda *used* to be like," he reminded his wife. "People do change, Joan. You did."

Miss Joan's eyes flashed as she angrily pointed out, "I was *never* anything like Zelda."

"I didn't say that that you were," Harry replied in an even voice. "I said you changed." To back up what he was saying, he explained, "There was a time when you swore you would never marry anyone ever again. And yet," he reminded her with an easy smile, "you did."

"That's different," Miss Joan snapped.

"Not really," Harry countered, then added, "Not to me. What I'm trying to point out, my love, is that Zelda paid for what she did. Paid for it dearly," he said insistently. "She deserves to be forgiven. Most of all, Eduardo deserves to have a second chance at being happy again and I think that your sister can make him happy. I honestly think that they can make each other happy," he emphasized. "But Zelda is not going to make a move if she thinks that doing so would be going against your wishes."

Miss Joan could see where this was going and she wasn't happy about it. She was even less happy that Harry was right…as he usually was.

"And if I don't agree?" Miss Joan challenged.

Harry knew the way his wife could be. But he didn't back down, and said, "I think you should."

Miss Joan made a face. "You know, there are times when I really regret ever having married you, Harry Monroe."

The corners of his eyes crinkled. "No, you don't," Harry told her with a confident smile.

Miss Joan frowned at him as she pointed toward the front of the establishment. "Get out of my diner, old man. I need to get it ready for the breakfast crowd that's about to descend on me."

"Will you tell Zelda that you're rescinding what you told her?" Harry asked, looking at his wife's face intently.

Miss Joan sighed deeply. "If it'll get you to stop lecturing me, yes, I'll tell her that I'm rescinding my decision."

"And you'll let her come with Eduardo to that party you're holding for 'Builder Boy'?" he asked, using the name he knew his wife used when referring to Jason.

Miss Joan's eyes narrowed again. "You're pushing it, old man."

"I know. But I know this wonderful woman who wisely taught me how to choose my battles…so I do," he told her with a wink.

Miss Joan frowned, pretending to be angry. "You know what I told you about talking to 'wonderful women.'"

Harry laughed as he leaned over and kissed his wife's cheek. "I know." He looked at Miss Joan one final time. "So you'll tell her?"

She closed her eyes as if she was searching for patience. "I'll tell her, I'll tell her. Now get out of here!" she ordered again.

Harry raised up his hands, as if in surrender. "Already gone."

"I don't know why I put up with you," Miss Joan told him, but there was just the smallest hint of a smile at the corners of her mouth as she said it.

"I don't know, either," he answered, amused, as he left the diner.

Miss Joan waited until she was certain that Harry had left the premises before she called toward the back office.

"Zelda! I need you to come out here!"

Zelda emerged, her eyes fixed on the freshly cleaned title floor. It was on the tip of her tongue to ask what she had done wrong now, but she refrained. The way Zelda saw it, she would find out what her transgression was soon enough. Right now, she was trying to figure out how she was going to tell Eduardo that she couldn't see him anymore without hurting his feelings.

There was a time when she would have stood up to her sister, but that had been before she had defied all rational thought and agreed to run off with Joan's husband. The baby, she realized almost immediately, had been collateral damage. She never stopped regretting what she had done.

Now she was determined to spend the rest of her life making it up to Joan. Even if her sister did forgive her, Zelda felt she would still wind up in arrears.

Zelda stood in the diner, waiting for her sister to finally say something.

Miss Joan drew in her breath. "It's come to my attention that I was letting certain things get the better of me," she said, measuring out her words slowly. "And that I was punishing not just you, but Eduardo, as well."

Stunned, Zelda continued to remain silent, staring at her sister.

Miss Joan frowned and pushed on. "So I've changed my mind. You can go back to seeing Eduardo again. And that party that's being given for Builder Boy this Saturday, you're welcome to come to that with Eduardo, too." She paused. When Zelda still remained silent, Miss Joan fixed her sister with an all but piercing look. "Well, aren't you going to say anything?"

Zelda raised her eyes toward her sister's face. "I'm waiting to wake up," she admitted quietly.

"You're not going to wake up, you ninny," Miss Joan informed her. "Because you're not asleep.

Now get back to filling those sugar shakers so we can open up for our customers."

Zelda allowed herself the slightest of smiles as she nodded vigorously. "Right away."

Miss Joan didn't even crack a smile. "Faster than that, Zelda," she ordered, walking over to check on the coffee urn.

It amazed Addie how quickly the work on the hospital was progressing. While gratifying, she strongly doubted that it had anything to do with her own participation on the job, although being good at what she did certainly did help, she thought happily.

And, although she would be the first to admit that Jason's leadership was rather impressive, the breathtaking progress on the hospital wasn't completely because of him, either. It had to do with the fact that the people who were working on every aspect of the hospital were all locals. The hospital they were outfitting, renovating and modernizing was extremely important to each and every one of them. Consequently, trying to complete it, especially ahead of schedule, meant everything to them.

The workers had been waiting for this hospital for what seemed like an eternity. To be part of this was nothing short of a miracle coming true.

Even though Addie was a realist, she looked forward to coming to work on a daily basis. Although tracking down hospital apparatus had its challenges, she definitely gave it her all. What Addie didn't understand, she researched. Every task she had undertaken since she had started this job, earlier in the week, had been a tremendous learning experience.

The more she learned, the better she got at her job.

She smiled to herself, satisfaction filtering through her entire being. She was getting very, *very* good at her job.

"Well, you certainly look pleased with yourself," Jason noted, checking in with Addie at the end of the day, as had become his habit in a very short matter of time.

"I am," Addie answered without any conceit. "I managed to track down one of the few remaining EEG machines for what turned out to be an extremely reasonable price." To prove her point, she held up the yellow pad in her hand confirming the price she had secured.

Jason glanced at it. "Impressive," he told her with a nod. "Maybe once this project becomes

history we can team up and work on the next hospital together so you can put what you learned on
this job to good use."

"Is that all you do?" The moment the words
were out of her mouth, Addie winced. That definitely didn't come out the way she had meant it.
"I didn't mean for it to sound like that," she apologized. "There is no 'all' when it comes to building a hospital."

Jason nodded, his expression the sheer picture
of neutrality. "As long as you know that." And then
the corners of his mouth curved.

"What?" Addie asked, wondering if she had
said something else that amused him without
meaning to.

"I'd say we're getting along pretty well,
wouldn't you?" Jason asked.

"I'd say the fact that I didn't try to choke you
the first day I met you bears testament to that,"
she replied.

"Can't just accept the win graciously, can you?"
Jason asked.

"I thought that was what I was doing," she answered. And then Addie laughed dryly. "This has
been a very long week," she pointed out. "I'm
sorry. I guess I'm a little short on graciousness
at the moment," Addie apologized, backtracking

out of a situation that could easily become volatile. "Have you given any thought as to what time you'd like to show up at the diner for the party tomorrow?"

"Why?" Jason asked. "Are you planning on having us show up at the party together?" he said, deadpan.

"No, I'm just being curious, that's all," Addie replied. She sighed, shaking her head. "Why do you make everything feel as if there's some sort of underlying consequences going on beneath whatever is being said?" she asked Jason impatiently.

He gave his answer some thought. "I guess that's just a result of my having to do business in some major cities. Landing a sought-after job in places like that always involves a great deal of competition." He shrugged. It was a given. "The one who manages to compete the best winds up winning."

Didn't the man know when to relax? "News flash—you've already landed the job. It's time to stop competing," Addie informed him.

Jason frowned. She was stating the obvious and he knew it. That didn't make it any easier to put up with.

"I know that," he answered shortly.

Her eyes met his. It was the end of the day.

Maybe she should just relax and let things go. By definition, tomorrow would be a good deal better.

Still, she couldn't resist continuing. "Maybe you should act like it and give the rest of us a break."

"By 'rest of us,' you mean you," Jason said, guessing at her real meaning.

"Well, I am part of 'us,'" she told him.

The way he smiled told her that she had managed to choose the right answer, even though it might have initially sounded like she might have put her foot in her mouth. Right now, she was much too tired to care.

"We'll start over again tomorrow," she said, then whirled around and began walking away.

"Noon," he called after her.

Addie stopped and turned around to look at the builder. "Excuse me?"

"I'll be going to the diner at noon tomorrow," he said. "To answer your previous question."

She nodded, pleased to have gotten an answer out of him. "I'll see you there then," she told him by way of parting.

"Yes," Jason murmured under his breath, "Count on it."

Chapter Twelve

"You're looking very dapper, Grandpa," Addie said, complimenting Eduardo the following morning when she walked into the living room. She slowly moved around him, scrutinizing the man.

"Do you think so?" he asked uncertainly, looking down at his pressed navy blue shirt and freshly laundered jeans. "I was not sure what to wear."

"Well, you certainly picked the right outfit, Grandpa. You look very handsome," she told him with a smile. "You had just better hope that Zelda isn't the jealous type because I can see a lot of ladies throwing themselves at you."

Eduardo frowned ever so slightly as he eyed her. "Now I know that you are just making fun of me."

But Addie only shook her head. "Never happen," she assured him. "Besides, you make your clothes look good, Grandpa, not the other way around."

Tickled by her comment, Eduardo laughed as he shook his head. "Where did you ever get that golden tongue of yours from?"

Her eyes shone as she answered, "I guess it just comes naturally."

Her grandfather looked at her with just a little bit of doubt. However he played along, anyway. "Most likely. By the way, you look very pretty— as always."

Addie pretended to shrug off the compliment, even though it secretly pleased her.

"It was just the first thing I grabbed out of my closet," she told him. Addie saw the skeptical look her grandfather gave her. "Well, maybe it was the second thing I grabbed."

"It is a very good choice," he said with approval.

"Are you going to be picking Zelda up and bringing her to the party?" Addie asked as she went to the kitchen. She poured herself a cup of coffee, then brought it back to the living room and sat down on the sofa.

"I am. Do you need a ride?" he asked, more than willing to bring his granddaughter along with him.

"Oh, I wouldn't want to cramp your style, Grandpa."

The phrase caught him off guard. "Cramp my style?" he echoed, confused.

"I wouldn't want to get in your way," she explained.

Eduardo waved a hand at her words. "You could never get in my way, little one," he insisted.

But Addie wasn't as sure as he was. "You never know, Grandpa. Zelda might want to be alone with you."

Now that she had accepted the fact that her grandfather was "keeping company," as she'd heard her grandfather's generation refer to dating someone, she wanted to make sure that he was comfortable with the situation.

Eduardo looked at her in all seriousness, then dismissed her suggestion. "Zelda knows how much my granddaughters mean to me. She would never want to come between us."

"And Ellie and I appreciate that," Addie responded with feeling. "But still, you definitely do deserve some alone time with Zelda, Grandpa. Now that Miss Joan has decided to back off and give both of you a little space, I would make good use of that situation if I were you."

Amused, Eduardo chuckled to himself. "You are a good girl, Addie."

Addie raised her chin. "I know," she replied. Only the twinkle in her eyes gave her away. "Now, I've got a few things to do before I'm ready to leave for the diner," she told him. She brushed her lips against his cheek. "I'll see you and your special lady there, Grandpa."

Grabbing her fringed shoulder bag, Addie headed out of the ranch house.

The new hospital she and the team had been working on for the last week seemed almost eerily quiet when Addie parked by the building and entered the premises. She had an idea for a commemorative gift for Jason and she needed to stop at the hospital-in-the-making before she headed to the diner.

Moving methodically around the first floor, which was amazingly taking shape at almost lightning speed, Addie took out her cell phone and began snapping a number of photographs of the area.

Satisfied that she had gotten a decent sampling for the album she was trying to create, Addie took out the small portable printer she had brought with her. She turned it on and aimed the camera at it.

In compliance, a number of four-by-six photographs came spewing out of the printer, one after another.

After retrieving the photographs, she quickly arranged them in order, then placed them in the small photo album she had brought with her. Once they were all tucked behind the plastic pages, Addie quickly looked over her project.

It made for a nice gift, she thought as she thumbed through the pages. Envisioning the hospital the way it would look when it was finally completed, she smiled to herself. The whole town would be proud of this since so many of the residents had had a hand in its construction.

Satisfied, Addie slipped the photo album into a small manila envelope and tucked the envelope into her shoulder bag. She should have thought to bring a ribbon or one of those ready-made bows, she thought, but it was too late now.

Jason didn't strike her as someone who needed bows, she decided.

When Addie pulled up to the parking lot next to the diner a few minutes later, she found that it was all but full. Obviously, a lot of people had decided to come to the party early. Her grandfather's white truck was already there.

She really hoped that Miss Joan hadn't decided to go back on her word. The woman had a way of making her displeasure known. And if Miss Joan did anything to make them feel uncomfortable—especially Zelda—she had a strong feeling that her grandfather wouldn't remain silent. He was a great believer in being a protector and she had seen the way he had looked at Zelda. Miss Joan's sister had a protector for life.

Because there were so many vehicles parked in the area, Addie had to drive farther down the street. The very first space she found, she parked her vehicle there.

She got out and quickly began to make her way back to Miss Joan's.

"I was beginning to think that you weren't coming."

Startled, Addie swung around, nearly hitting Jason with her shoulder bag. She pulled it back at the last second as she found herself looking up into his face.

Addie blinked. She had just assumed that if Jason had arrived at Miss Joan's diner, he would have gone in, not lingered out here.

"Were you waiting for me?" she asked him in disbelief.

"Actually, I was," he admitted, seeing no point in playing games. "By the way, thanks for not hitting me with your purse."

She was still trying to process what was going on. "Did I forget that we made arrangements to attend this celebration together?" As far as she knew, they hadn't, but then she had been tired last night, and it might have just slipped her mind.

"No, we didn't," he told her, then added, "But I thought it might be a good idea if I went into the diner with someone who Miss Joan liked."

That didn't make any sense to her. "Miss Joan's throwing this party in your honor," Addie reminded him.

"That doesn't necessarily mean that she likes me," Jason pointed out. He knew a lot of people who did things for others because it looked good.

Addie stopped walking and glanced at the man beside her. "Let me tell you something about Miss Joan. That woman *never* does anything that she doesn't want to do. *Never*," she said with emphasis.

"Still, you'll forgive me if I think I would fare better with you at my side," Jason said.

Addie couldn't help thinking that notion had a

nice ring to it. The corners of her mouth curved. "I think I can put up with that."

Stopping on the top step, Jason opened the diner door. He moved to one side, holding the door open for Addie as she walked in.

Addie scanned the immediate area. She saw a lot of people she recognized, but her eyes were drawn to Miss Joan. No matter where she was, the woman always seemed to assume center stage.

For her part, the town matriarch was looking their way. Specifically, Miss Joan was eying Jason. She nodded her head at them in a silent greeting.

Miss Joan cut across the floor and reached the couple. "I was beginning to think you had lost your way," she said to Jason.

"I was waiting for Addie," he told Miss Joan.

"Why?" the woman asked. "You were here a good half an hour before Addie arrived."

Stunned, Jason stared at the woman and then shook his head in sheer amazement. "Is there anything that you don't know?" he asked her.

Miss Joan smiled at the guest of honor. "When I come up with an answer to that," she told him, "I'll let you know." She inclined her head toward the two of them, moving on. "Meanwhile, what are you drinking?"

It was Addie's turn to be amazed. "You're serving drinks, Miss Joan?" she asked. Alcohol was not something to be found on the diner's menu.

"The Murphy brothers offered to supply us with beverages for the evening's festivities," Miss Joan told her, glancing over her thin shoulder toward the oldest member of the clan, Brett Murphy. "Now, what will you have?"

This was a little early in the day for him, Jason thought. But he had a feeling that refusing the woman's hospitality would undoubtedly be constituted as bad form, so he said, "I'll have a shot of tequila."

Miss Joan nodded. "And you?" she asked Addie.

Addie said the first thing that came to mind. "I'll have a margarita."

Miss Joan pointed toward the rear of the diner. "The bar's set up in the back," she said, then urged, "Place your orders. And help yourselves to the buffet."

With that, the woman made her way toward the latest batch of guests who had just made their way into the diner.

"Where are all these people going to sit?" Jason asked as they got their drinks, thinking that Addie had to have some sort of insight in the matter since this couldn't be the first party that Miss Joan had thrown.

"For the most part, they'll probably stand," she told him. "And Miss Joan has tables and folding chairs placed outside in the back for those who wanted to sit down when they have their meal, or just socialize."

"That sounds very organized," Jason commented. He was a huge fan of organization, since chaos had a way of costing time and money.

Addie laughed. "You don't know the half of it. For as long as I've known her, Miss Joan has *always* been exceedingly organized. It's one of the reasons she's been in charge of the annual hunt for the town Christmas tree." Because Jason actually looked interested, she gave him details. "Miss Joan picks several people to go bring back this huge tree each year. They put it up in the town square and then it's decorated. Everyone in town takes part in that, from the youngest to the oldest," Addie explained as she sipped her margarita.

"Miss Joan also pays for everything," she added. "It's not just about ordering people around and hearing the sound of her own voice," Addie pointed out, knowing what had to be going through his mind.

Jason thoughtfully glanced over at Miss Joan as she wove her way around the diner. "So I'm beginning to learn," he said more to himself than to Addie.

Addie nodded. She couldn't resist reminding him of the woman's place in Forever. "She's a really good person to know, especially when you find yourself in a bind."

"Wouldn't that make her feel as if she was being used?" Jason asked.

"No, it doesn't," Addie answered. "Miss Joan likes being useful…in her own unique way," she explained.

Jason nodded. "So I see," he replied.

The diner was growing more and more crowded. Instinctively, he took hold of Addie's arm to guide her over to the large side table, where a great many of the various items that comprised the buffet had been arranged.

Addie thought of telling Jason that she was perfectly capable of making her way across the floor herself, but somehow, saying as much struck her as being unnecessarily combative. At this point, she decided to take Jason's guiding her toward the buffet in the spirit it was intended—just out-and-out helpfulness.

Addie gestured toward the bountiful table and asked, "So what's your pleasure."

The word *you* unexpectedly flashed through his mind in big, bold letters. It took him completely aback, especially since he realized that it was true.

Jason paused, trying to mentally regroup as he stared at the contents of the table.

There were slices of baked ham as well as rare roast beef and brisket. There were also servings of shrimp scampi and a number of other choices, too.

And, of course, he noted with a smile, individual servings of chicken pot pie.

The woman really knew how to put on a spread, he thought.

"I really don't know where to start," Jason said honestly.

He didn't want to appear to be greedy, but he had to admit that everything looked really, really tempting and appetizing.

Addie noticed Jason's indecisiveness. She offered her advice. "Why don't you take a small helping of a few of the items?" she suggested. "That way, you might find something that really appeals to you, or discover something that you didn't even know you liked. Angel has a really great way with recipes."

He nodded, thinking back to the first meal he'd had at the diner. "So I've discovered," he said. Picking two plates, he looked at Addie. "And what can I get for you?"

"I'm going to let the margarita settle down first, and then I'm going to get a helping of prime rib and mashed potatoes…and maybe a serving of chicken pot pie."

Jason smiled. "You know what? That sounds

really good. You've got my mouth watering," he admitted. Turning toward Dolores, the server that Miss Joan had left in charge of this particular buffet, Jason told the woman, "We'll each have a serving of prime rib, mashed potatoes and an individual chicken pot pie." He watched the woman's face to see if he had gone overboard.

But Dolores just smiled broadly. "Those are my favorites, too. Coming right up, Mr. Eastwood."

While he was accustomed to being addressed by his surname on the worksite, somehow it just didn't seem right to hear himself referred to that way at a party being thrown in his honor. Especially when everyone seemed to be so friendly with everyone else.

He needed to rethink things, Jason told himself, and approach them from a different angle. Being called by his given name rather than by his surname didn't make him any less in charge, he decided. As a matter of fact, it made things a little more relaxed.

He liked the idea of a relaxed workplace.

"You can call me Jason," he told Dolores.

The young server's smile rose to her eyes as she replied, "Yes, sir, I'll be sure to do that." And then she went on to give them each a large serving of prime rib and mashed potatoes and an individual chicken-pot-pie tin.

Chapter Thirteen

Everyone seemed to feel that this was the best party that Miss Joan had ever given. It had been going on now for close to nine hours. All the town residents had put in an appearance at one point or another. Some for a short while, while others had stayed the entire time.

Various servings of food also made an appearance. They were no sooner brought out than they disappeared, replaced by other dishes.

Moreover, Jason discovered that he had a great deal more in common with the woman he had come to think of as his assistant than he'd thought he did.

He was also really touched by the small album of photos of the hospital-in-progress she had put together for him. It was a first for him. No one had ever even thought of doing something like that before.

"I'll hang on to this," he told her and Addie got the feeling that he wasn't just mouthing empty words. She was glad she had thought of it.

During the festivities, Jason also found that he got along with the local workers on a personal level a great deal better than he had initially believed he would. Up until now, his entire background had been grounded in medicine and specifically the building of hospitals, but somehow, this was different. Happily, common ground could still be forged.

And, as Jason talked to the locals, as well as to Addie, he ate.

And ate.

"I think I finally ate too much," Jason confessed as he pushed away yet another empty plate. In deference to his full stomach, he had finally given in and sat down in one of the booths, stretching his legs out before him as if that could somehow distribute the calories he had consumed more evenly.

Addie took the seat opposite him and smiled understandingly. Unlike Jason, even though she enjoyed it, she had consumed the food being served in moderation.

"So what was your first clue?" she teased Jason.

He looked down at his waist. His pants had never felt this tight before. "The fact that the top button on my pants feels like it might just go shooting off at any second like some sort of a bullet."

"You could try unbuttoning your pants," Addie suggested with a smile.

But Jason shook his head. "I'd better not. If I so much as touch that button, it could very well make a hole in something."

Addie's eyes crinkled. "Thanks for the warning," she joked. "I'll make sure to stay out of range. Actually," she told him, looking at his plate, "I'm really surprised that you were able to get that much down. Although," she continued, "I have to admit that Angel's cooking is really, really hard to resist."

"Not to mention that I always eat a lot," Jason confided. "But I think that this time I finally overdid it." He rested his hand on his stomach, as if that could somehow get it to settle down. It couldn't. "I don't usually get this full."

She had been watching Jason over the course of the last few hours and had to admit that she was rather amazed that he was able to pack it away the way he had.

"Why aren't you three times your size?" she asked. By all rights, she thought, he should have been.

Jason laughed dryly. He was lucky, he supposed. "Mostly because having a metabolism like a shrew runs in my family," he admitted. "We work hard, we play hard and, consequently, we eat hard to sustain ourselves."

She couldn't argue with that, she thought. "Well, you certainly won Miss Joan's heart," Addie told him.

Jason didn't see how that was even remotely possible. "With all these people milling around in the diner—and outside—how could Miss Joan possibly even keep tabs on what I consumed?" he asked.

"Because "

Jason interrupted Addie and finished her statement. "She's Miss Joan. Yes, I'm beginning to get that," Jason admitted, although for the life of him, he had no idea how the older woman managed to pull off her particular brand of voodoo the way that she did.

Addie continued to study him across the table. "Something you want to say?" Jason asked, curious.

"You know, you are looking a wee bit uncomfortable," she said now that she thought about it.

Jason didn't take any offense at her observation. Instead, he laughed shortly. "Consuming my weight in food might have something to do with that," he admitted.

Searching for a solution, Addie looked around the diner. "Why don't we go out for a walk and get a breath of fresh air?" she suggested. "Moving around, plus the night air, might make you feel a little less stuffed."

At this point, Jason was willing to try anything. "I'm open to that," he told her. He doubted that he could feel any more stuffed than he did.

As they headed for the door, Jason could have sworn he felt Miss Joan following them with her eyes.

Noting the look on the woman's face, Addie said to her, "We're just going out for a short walk and a breath of fresh air, Miss Joan. We'll be back in a few minutes."

Jason added in his piece, thinking what he said made it sound more realistic.

"I need to burn up some of these excess calories so I can make room for more," he told the woman. "Everything is just too good to resist."

"I'm sure Angel will be very happy to hear that," Miss Joan said to him, but it was obvious that Angel would not be the only one who was glad to hear what the evening's guest of honor had to say.

As for Addie, she kept her comment to herself until she and Jason had made it out the door. And then she looked at Jason. There was no missing her pleased expression.

"You're learning how to talk to Miss Joan," she said, congratulating him.

Jason nodded and laughed. "I have fairly decent survival instincts. They just take a while to kick in," he admitted as they went down the front steps. "But they are pretty good," he acknowledged. "Although I have to admit, Miss Joan is really in a class by herself."

"She's growing on you, isn't she?" Addie asked, reminding him what she had predicted about the woman earlier.

Jason nodded. "I guess she is at that," he acknowledged.

The cool night air rustled around them, sending the leaves moving about rather noisily. "So where do you want to go?" he asked Addie.

She shrugged, gesturing about the area vaguely. "Just around."

Jason found that he had to strain to concentrate in order to look around and attempt to make things out. By his estimation, he had been in Forever for a while now and he still hadn't gotten used to the fact that away from the diner and a few other sources of light—such as Murphy's—at night the area really looked pitch-black.

"How do you get used to it?" Jason asked her. "The darkness," he explained when he realized that Addie had tilted her head in his direction and was giving him a quizzical look.

"Oh, it's not always so dark," Addie assured the builder.

"Yeah, in the daytime, there's the sun," he deadpanned.

Addie watched him patiently. "I wasn't talking about that. Some of the time," she went on, "there's a full moon out and that casts a lot of light."

"But most of the time, there isn't a full moon," he reminded her. "Like when there's a new moon out and the area is pitch-black."

"Oh, I don't know. That can be pretty romantic at times," she pointed out. "Haven't you ever been out with a woman and wished that the surrounding area wasn't quite as brightly lit as it was?" she asked as she turned toward him. "In a way, the darkness makes people bolder. It gives them permission to do things that they might not be brave enough to attempt to do in the light of day."

By now, they had reached the far end of the

parking lot and had stopped walking. There was a half moon out—not enough to illuminate the area, but just enough to highlight a part of it.

Addie could *feel* Jason breathing more than she could actually see him doing it.

And then he moved closer toward her. As if on cue, her heart began pounding. Jason slowly reached out to frame her face. Addie anticipated what was going to happen next.

She stood very, very still.

What came next happened almost in slow motion.

Jason bent over her and then his lips covered hers. Addie's breath caught in her throat while her heart went on pounding.

Wildly.

The explosion that immediately followed between them left her completely breathless. She wasn't actually aware of raising up on her toes, couldn't remember if Jason pressed his body against hers or if she was the one who pressed hers against his.

There just seemed to be a mutual bonding that occurred between them.

A single word—*wow*—echoed in Addie's brain. Or maybe it was the word *more*, but it definitely echoed.

After an endless moment, still in awe, Addie drew back and looked up at Jason. She did her best to make out his features.

"I guess you were right about the darkness," Jason whispered, his words all but vibrating along her skin. "I don't think that I would have been able to do that in the light of day," he confessed.

Addie did her best to make light of the moment. "That's because the darkness hides flaws," she told him.

"Mine?" he guessed. "Because in case I haven't made it very obvious," he said to her, wondering how she would feel if he kissed her again, "I don't think that you have any. At least, not any physical ones."

She wasn't sure if she followed him. Was he complimenting her, or bring brutally honest? "Meaning?"

Jason grinned. He felt that being honest with her was the only way they would be able to make any progress. "I noticed that you can be a little pushy, but then I think you might already know that."

"You know," she said, her eyes holding his, "if you weren't such a good kisser, this is the part where I'd be tempted to give you a good swift kick."

Jason zeroed in on what he felt was the only

important part. "So you think I'm a good kisser?" he asked, pleased.

Her eyebrows drew together as she stared at Jason. "Did you miss the rest of what I just said?" Addie asked.

Jason inclined his head. "Conveniently, yes," he answered, the smile on his face widening.

With that, he drew Addie gently back into his arms. His intent was to kiss her again, this time with even more fervor than he had the first time.

There was no doubt about it—she did make his blood rush.

He honestly couldn't have said where this situation might have progressed to if the sound of car doors being slammed shut hadn't echoed from the end of the parking lot.

Hearing the doors, Addie and Jason dropped their arms from one another and instantly stepped back as if the kiss between them had never even happened.

Addie blew out a shaky breath, then ventured a look to her side to see if they had even been detected.

And, if they had, by whom.

She looked at the vehicle that was driving out of the lot and, belatedly, she recognized a late-model SUV. Addie smiled. She had a feeling that they hadn't been spotted, otherwise the owners would have called out to them.

"Those were the Hendersons," she informed Jason.

"And?" At the moment, the name meant nothing to him.

"And they have a carload of kids," she told him. "Their kids are at the stage where they all still talk at once, so our secret is safe," Addie said.

"Our secret?" he asked. "What secret is that?"

She gave him a look. "That you kissed me."

"I thought we kissed each other," Jason said, amused by the way she had phrased what had just happened between them.

She wasn't about to argue about who had initiated the kiss. What mattered was that it had happened.

Addie decided that it was best to treat the whole thing lightly.

"Potato, po-tat-o," she said. "I just thought you'd be more comfortable that what just happened between us remained a secret no matter who had set the wheels in motion."

Jason laughed, shaking his head. "You do have a rather unique way of phrasing things. And what makes you think that I'd be embarrassed by the fact that you kissed me?" he asked Addie innocently. He saw the look that entered her eyes and shook his head. "I guess the darkness robbed you of your sense of humor," he said.

"My sense of humor is alive and well and perfectly intact…if there was something to laugh at," she informed the builder.

And then, unable to keep a straight face any longer, Addie laughed. "I think that maybe we'd be better off if we just put this all behind us by Monday morning."

Maybe it was all that food he had consumed, or perhaps it was the two shots of tequila, but there was a sparkle in his eyes as he archly asked Addie, "What do you suggest we do with it until then?"

"Then you do have a sense of humor," Addie declared, pretending to be amazed.

Jason ran the crook of his index finger against her cheek. He could have sworn that a spark of electricity ran between them at that moment.

"When there's something to laugh at," he replied softly.

"I think we should get back to the diner before Miss Joan sends a posse to come looking for us," Addie told him.

Taking his hand in hers, she began to lead the way back…or started to. When Jason made no move to follow her lead, Addie turned to look at him, a silent question in her eyes.

"In a minute," he replied.

She didn't understand. "What's going to happen in a minute?" she asked.

"This," he replied softly.

And a moment later, he kissed her again.

Soundly, sending every nerve ending in her body undulating.

When he finally separated his lips from hers, Addie felt as if every inch of her body—not just her lips—was tingling.

It took her a second to draw enough air into her lungs to be able to form words, and another second after that for the words to sound logical.

"Are we ready to go back now?" Addie asked, rather surprised that she was able to say anything coherent.

Her head felt as if all the thoughts inside it were being scrambled.

Jason wanted to say "no," that he wanted to remain right here and go on kissing her, but that would undoubtedly lead to trouble, and while that might not be a bad way to go down, now was not the time.

It was much too early.

So he replied, "Yes," even though he felt as if the actual reply was "no."

They made the short trip back to the diner in silence, a silence that was immediately broken the moment that they walked back in through the diner door.

Miss Joan instantly looked their way, as if she had been waiting for their return all along. The look on the woman's face spoke volumes, even though, for once, not a single word passed from her lips.

She merely smiled knowingly at them before she turned toward one of the Murphy brothers. "I think it's time you brought out the champagne," she told Brett.

As usual, there was no debating with Miss Joan's tone.

He had brought several bottles with him and they were currently on ice.

"Right away, Miss Joan," he told her as he went to fetch the bottles.

Chapter Fourteen

Addie didn't know just what to expect the following Monday morning. She hadn't spoken to Jason since the party had finally wrapped up at the diner late that Saturday night.

That was one of the reasons that she decided to go in early and get a head start on the day. And she also wanted to talk to a new hospital-equipment dealer. She had managed to track down two brand-new CAT-scan machines, which were being sold at an exceedingly reasonable price, far lower than anything else she had been able to locate.

She'd been hired to work on the hospital's inner

structure, but now, at least half her time was taken up by what seemed like a scavenger hunt. The money paying for all these machines was not coming out of her own pocket, of course, but Addie couldn't help feeling that the more she was able to save paying for all this equipment, the better the chances were of getting more machines for the hospital.

She had quickly discovered that there were myriad items involved when it came to stocking a hospital, even a smaller hospital like this one. Addie felt that the more items that they could manage to purchase at less than cost, the better hospital they were putting together.

The problem, she now discovered, was that there was another organization looking to purchase a new CAT-scan machine for their hospital.

The supplier she had located who dealt in CAT-scan machines was impressed that she was in so early on a Monday morning. He had agreed to let her make her pitch for the CAT scan—or rather two CAT scans—before the other hospital. The only drawback was that the dealer was located on the outside of Dallas.

She needed to get there fast. If Ellie had returned from her honeymoon, getting there quickly wouldn't have presented a problem. But as it was, it did. She would have to drive, instead of fly in her sister's plane.

Addie threw together all the communications that had gone on between her and the medical-equipment store owner. Putting them in a folder, she then double-checked that she had the project's checkbook as well as her GPS. Hurrying out of the small cubbyhole that was now doubling as her office on the premises, Addie all but collided with Jason, who had chosen that moment to walk in.

Surprised, Jason grabbed hold of Addie's shoulders to prevent her from falling backward. Holding on tightly, he managed to steady her enough so that she could regain her balance.

"Where are you off to so early in such a big hurry?" he asked.

The pleasant sensation that filtered through him because he was holding her again was not lost on Jason.

Releasing her after a beat, he whimsically asked, "Did you get a better offer?"

She had honestly thought that she could get out and be on the road before Jason came in to work. The kisses they had shared in the dark the other night had left a very real impression on Addie, and she wanted a little more time to go by before she felt she could face the repercussions of what had happened between them.

Obviously, that wasn't going to happen, she thought.

"Yes," she said, answering his question. "But it's not what you think," she stressed, seeing the look that came into his eyes. "I managed to get a really good price on a couple of brand-new CAT-scan machines. There's another buyer who's interested so I have to get there first to lay the groundwork for the buy."

Truthfully, Addie expected some sort of sarcastic remark from Jason in response. But the look on his face told her that he actually appeared to be rather impressed.

"Where is this place?" he asked

"It's located on the edge of Dallas," she answered. She decided to give Jason a little background information to convince him. "The owner recently took the company over from his late father and he's eager to make his own mark," she explained. "The new owner, Albert Hobbs, is also sympathetic to people attempting to stock a new hospital, so I've got that going for me, but I really need to get going now," Addie insisted. "He has an appointment with another buyer later this afternoon."

Listening, Jason nodded, then asked, "Who's going with you?"

"Nobody," she told him, wondering why he would even ask that. "I made sure everyone had their assignments and, quite honestly, nobody can be spared for this little field trip."

"Except you," Jason said.

Well, somebody had to do it, she thought. "I am the one who found the deal in the first place and I think I can finish the job by pushing it over the finish line."

Jason nodded. Holding up his hand, he told her, "Give me a minute."

She wanted to ask what he needed a minute for, but she decided that questioning the man who was overseeing the entire operation wouldn't be in her best interest, so she nodded. Stepping back into the office, she glanced at her watch, calculating just how much time she was losing by being cooperative when she was supposed to be getting on the road.

When Jason finished making his phone call, he crossed the floor back to her.

"Okay, all settled," he told Addie. "Let's go."

He couldn't mean what she thought he meant. "Go where?" she asked him suspiciously.

"According to you, to see a man about a couple

of CAT-scan machines," he answered. "What did you think I meant?"

She stared at him, still trying to process what he had just said. "You're coming with me?" she asked.

"I'm the guy in charge of the budget, not to mention ultimately the whole project. Why do you look so stunned?" he asked.

"Because you *are* the guy who's in charge of everything," she told Jason. "You can't just go running off to take care of every single little detail."

"How much money do you think the hospital will save if you can get this guy to sell those two CAT scans to us?" he asked Addie.

Crossing her fingers behind her back, she quoted him a price, hoping it wouldn't go up by the time they reached the store.

The quote she gave Jason earned an appreciative whistle from him. "I'd say that's definitely worth the trip. That phone call I just made was to make sure that I've got all my bases covered. Now, do you want to stand here and go on talking, or do you want to get going?" he asked her.

"The latter," she answered, hurrying toward the door.

"Too bad that Ellie and my cousin are still on their honeymoon," Jason commented. "Otherwise, she could have flown us to that company in Dallas."

"Us," she repeated as they walked into the makeshift parking lot. "Then you'd still want to come?" Addie asked, surprised.

"Sure. Nothing's changed except our mode of transportation," Jason said.

Outside the building, he pointed toward his van. "We're taking my vehicle," he told her. Then, guessing that Addie probably wanted a reason for his decision, he said, "If nothing else, it's probably more comfortable."

"Comfort wasn't my first concern," she told him, striding toward the van. "I was focusing on speed."

A thought occurred to him. "Why, is the other company coming to bid on the CAT-scan machines early?"

"I honestly don't know if they are or not," she told him as she put her hand on the passenger-side handle. "But I'm not about to take a chance." When she tried to open it, the door didn't budge. She tried a second time, then Jason hit the button on his key fob. All four locks sprang open. "You lock your car?" she asked him in amazement.

"Yes. Why?" he asked, getting in and buckling

his seat belt. "Don't you?" He waited for her to get in and buckle hers.

"Around here," she told him, "we trust our neighbors. Everyone knows that if anyone tries anything, Miss Joan would ban them from the diner if they were older. Or, if they're kids, she'd tan their hides," Addie explained.

He wasn't sure if he totally believed that, but for now, he decided to go along with Addie's narrative. "Must be nice to have rules that are that simple." Putting his key into the ignition, he looked at Addie. "You do have the address, right?"

"No, I thought I'd just drive around once we got to Dallas and hope that we'd stumble across the company." She gave him an annoyed look for asking. "Yes, I have the address," she informed him, then rattled it off in case he was going to challenge her.

"Sorry," he apologized as he drove off. "I didn't mean to insult you."

"You're forgiven. But if we're going to go on working together—successfully—we're going to have to set down some ground rules," Addie informed him.

Jason glanced at her before looking back at the road. "I thought we already had," he told her with a smile.

Addie had a feeling that Jason had to be talking about what had happened between them on Saturday night. She was not about to get into that first thing Monday morning. Possibly not for a while, not until she knew how she felt about the matter.

"Take the next right," she directed, changing the topic altogether. "That'll lead you to the expressway."

Okay, back to business, Jason thought. Just as well for now, he decided. "Got it."

They made the trip in record time, which was a good thing because as it turned out, Albert Hobbs, the new owner of Stay Healthy, the company that owned the CAT-scan machines they were coming to purchase—as well as several other machines— was just on his way out.

"Mr. Hobbs?" Addie asked, presenting herself right in front of the man.

Just about to lock his shop door, he looked at her quizzically. "Yes?"

"I'm Addie Montenegro," she said, putting out her hand to him. "We spoke on the phone early this morning."

Hobbs looked rather surprised, then impressed as he allowed himself a smile. "I didn't think you'd be here this fast…or that you were this young," he added.

Jason felt a surprising slight prick of jealousy before he managed to block it and lock it away.

"I never say anything I don't mean," Addie told the store owner, echoing Miss Joan's mantra. Remembering that she wasn't alone, she gestured toward Jason. "Mr. Hobbs, this is Jason Eastwood, the man who's in charge of building Forever's hospital." She waited until the two men shook hands, then cheerfully continued. "Now, let's talk CAT scans."

Stay Healthy's company president looked more than very willing to do just that.

Addie was happy to discover that negotiations went rather quickly. To her relief, there was no last-minute dickering, no attempts to jack up the price. Instead, Hobbs led them to one of the back rooms to look at the machines.

"And they work?" Jason asked after he and Addie carefully examined the machines. There was a bit of suspicion in his voice. "That is a pretty low price you quoted," he commented.

"I can increase it," Hobbs offered pleasantly.

Addie quickly stepped in. "No, that's all right." She cast a glance in Jason's direction. "It's just that normally he's used to CAT scans being priced a lot higher."

It was obvious that Hobbs was still adjusting to his new position...but he was getting there. "My dad always had a soft spot in his heart for start-up companies. I grant you that there aren't that many around, but once in a while, one does show up. When you said that your town only had six hundred people and were engaged in ambitiously building your own hospital, I knew you were the kind of people who would have appealed to my dad." He smiled ruefully. "The man would haunt me if I passed up the opportunity to help you out. Luckily, I was able to get my hands on some machines at cost so I can pass that on to you," Hobbs told them.

Addie spoke up before Jason could say anything. "The people of Forever will be in your debt, Mr. Hobbs," she assured the man.

Hobbs nodded. "I learned a long time ago to just pay it forward," he said, looking at the duo. "I expect that you will go on to do the same," he told them.

Jason was accustomed to business taking a long time to be conducted when it came to finally closing in on a price. This, however, was done in what amounted to record time. It amazed him. In the end, everyone wound up pleased.

By two o'clock, Addie and Jason were back on the road, both CAT-scan machines carefully packed in the back of the gunmetal-gray van.

Confident that the machines were carefully secured, Addie breathed a heartfelt sigh of relief.

That was when she realized that Jason hadn't spoken a word since they had pulled away from the shop.

"You're being awfully quiet," Addie observed once they were on the road back to Forever.

He glanced at her. "I was just thinking about what an asset you turned out to be," Jason told her. "When I agreed to having you work on building the hospital, I had no idea what you were actually capable of. I mean, Neil told me that you were really handy with a hammer, but I just thought he was being kind about his future wife's sister. I had no idea you could actually *build* things. And I certainly didn't know that you were a wheeler-dealer, as well." He had been thinking about this since they'd met the store owner. "Today was really impressive. Once this hospital is finished, I could certainly use you on my next project."

Staring at Jason, for once Addie was rendered

speechless. When she finally spoke, she cried, "You're serious."

"I believe the old saying is 'as serious as a heart attack' but I honestly never cared for that comparison," Jason admitted.

Her mouth curved. "Well, we have that in common," Addie told him.

"But, nevertheless, I am serious about you coming to work for me once this project is finished," he told her.

"Always looking to the next job, is that it?" she asked.

"Sure," Jason answered. "After all, what else is there?"

She felt like he'd put her on the spot, but since he'd asked, she had to speak her mind. "Oh, I don't know. Did you ever consider settling down?"

He shrugged. "That's just another way of saying stagnating."

"Is that how you really feel?" she asked.

"Let's just say I like facing a challenge. Once a job is done, there has to be something new on the horizon to pique my interest."

Addie decided to step away from the conversation for now. Anything she said might get her in trouble.

"I realize that right now, the job is still ongoing

and will be for some time to come," she mused. "It might be good for the project—and the people involved—to just focus on that for the moment. The future has a habit of taking care of itself."

"That's a good point," he agreed. "So are we done here or do you have anywhere else that you want to stop?"

"We have what we came for," she told him. "My next hunt is for several more chest X-ray machines. And it wouldn't hurt to get a couple of mammogram machines." He could all but see the wheels whirling in her head. "As well as ultrasound equipment."

"I see that you've been doing your homework," Jason commented.

She looked at him, bracing herself for a confrontation. Apparently, he wasn't the type who believed in letting sleeping dogs lie.

"Does that surprise you?" Addie asked.

But Jason merely shook his head. In his estimation, this had been a very good day, thanks to Addie.

"No," he freely admitted, smiling at her. "Not really."

Chapter Fifteen

A routine was quickly solidified. By the time a few weeks had gone by, after working a ten-to-twelve-hour day, Jason and Addie would finally knock off and go have dinner at Miss Joan's diner. During dinner, they would unwind and, more than likely, compare notes as to how things at the hospital were progressing.

Jason couldn't have been more amazed—or pleased—to find this sort of common ground.

"You know," Jason told Addie as they walked into the diner, crossed to the counter and took their seats, "I think this has to be the most progress I've ever made on a job in such a short amount of time."

"That's because each and every person involved in this project has a great deal invested in getting this hospital up and on its feet. It's a labor of love, so to speak," Addie explained. "Everyone has been waiting a very long time for Forever to get its own hospital, something beyond the clinic that Dr. Davenport reopened when he came to take his late brother's place in Forever."

Little by little, Jason was learning the history of this small town that had become the location of his most recent project.

"You're probably right," Jason said, nodding his head.

"Oh, I know I am," Addie told him. "And before you make a comment about my being conceited, I happen to know the people who live here. How they think, what's important to them. That's why I know they've thrown themselves into this project and are working as hard as they are."

"I wasn't about to say anything sarcastic," Jason told her. The corners of his mouth curved as he studied her. "In the last few weeks, I've gotten to have a very healthy respect for those instincts of yours."

She blew out a breath. "Well, you've definitely taken the wind out of my sails," Addie admitted.

Jason met her statement with a hearty laugh. "I didn't think that was even possible," he told her. "I'd call that a miracle."

"Well, you two seem to be in a good mood," Miss Joan observed as she made her way toward the duo. "I take it that work on the hospital is going well," she said dryly.

Jason nodded, happy to be the bearer of positive news. "Better than expected, as well as ahead of schedule."

For a moment, Miss Joan appeared to be a little skeptical. But then she nodded. "That's nice to hear."

Jason had learned how to flatter Miss Joan and how to lightly stroke the woman's ego. "It must be all that good food the workers get here at the diner that energizes them."

Miss Joan arched a thinly shaped eyebrow. "Laying it on a little thick, aren't you, Builder Boy?" she asked.

Jason was the picture of innocence as he said to the woman, "I'm just calling it the way I see it, Miss Joan. I've worked on a number of projects over the years, and none of those projects ever made this sort of progress this fast, so my guess is that it has to be due to the food. At least in part," he qualified with a smile.

Giving him a dubious look, Miss Joan pressed her lips together. "Sweet-talking me isn't going to get you anywhere, Builder Boy," she told him.

"I wasn't trying to sweet-talk you, Miss Joan. Just stating a fact," Jason answered honestly.

Miss Joan uttered an impatient noise, then informed the pair, "Angel just whipped up some fresh pork loin. She did it in the last hour just before the end of her shift. Let me see if there's any left," she told Jason, sparing a glance toward Addie.

Addie was convinced that the woman had no need to check. "She probably put some aside for you," she told Jason once Miss Joan had gone toward the kitchen. And then she nodded and smiled at him. "You certainly seem to have won her over. Congratulations."

The way he saw it, one compliment deserved another. "I just took your advice to heart," he said with a shrug.

The look on Addie's face appeared rather doubtful. "Well, that's a first," she murmured. In truth, Addie wouldn't have thought that the builder had actually paid that much attention to anything she had to say.

"Not really," Jason contradicted. "I always make it a point to listen to good advice and take it to heart whenever I can," he informed her. "And you give good advice."

Talk about laying it on thick, Addie thought, recalling what Miss Joan had said about what Jason had said earlier. "And where is this going?"

"Nowhere." He drew his hands apart in an innocent shrug. "I'm just answering your question," he told her. "You know, I would have never guessed that you were such a suspicious woman."

Her eyes met his and just the faintest of smiles curved her lips. "Must be the company I keep," she responded.

"You're in luck," Miss Joan announced as she returned to the counter carrying a tray in front of her. She set down the tray between them. "I have no idea why, but it seems that Angel set aside two servings of her pork loin just before she left for the day." Miss Joan placed the two plates in front of them, then gave Jason a warning look. "I wouldn't get used to this sort of thing if I were you," the woman told them.

"Absolutely not," Jason promised, keeping his voice solemn, which was a dead giveaway as to how he felt. "I'm just grateful it happened," he said to the woman innocently.

Miss Joan stared at him for a moment, then shifted her eyes toward Addie. "I'd be careful around this one if I were you."

"Why?" Addie asked, trying her best to hide her amusement.

"Well, for one thing, his nose is liable to grow at any second and you'll wind up tripping over it." She nodded toward the dinner plates that also contained servings of bread-crumb-covered green beans and baked potatoes with a healthy serving of toppings. "All right, eat your dinner before it gets cold," she said to Jason before walking away again.

"That's the second time she's said that to me," Jason observed.

"You're actually keeping count?" Addie asked, surprised.

"It's not that," Jason answered. "It's just that my own mother never said anything like that to me. It leaves an impression."

She tried to find an explanation that didn't point to his mother being disinterested in Jason's activities. "Maybe you just never allowed anything to get cold," Addie suggested

But Jason knew better. "No, it's not that. Both of my parents were surgeons and at least half the time, they were away, performing surgeries or checking on their patients after the surgeries were performed." He laughed softly under his breath. "When I was a kid, I thought that they cared more about their patients than they cared about me. When I got older, I was proud of them. But as a kid, your thinking takes a selfish bent."

Her heart went out to Jason. "That's understandable," she said sympathetically.

He appreciated the effort, but he wasn't buying it. "You're just saying that," he told her, waving a hand at her words.

"No, I'm not," she insisted, digging in. "All kids want to be the center of their parents' world," she told him. She remembered her own childhood and how lonely she had felt at times. "I would have given *anything* to have parents who thought of me as the center of their universe. I would have given anything to have parents. But, on the positive side, I was just grateful that Ellie and I had a loving grandfather who was there for us.

"But that didn't mean that I liked being disciplined or having to do chores as a kid," she added quickly. "We really do see things differently when we're the center of our own universe. You said your parents were surgeons. Did they want you to become a doctor?"

"As a matter of fact," Jason admitted, "they did."

She wondered if there had been arguments over

that. "What did they say when you told them you were going to be a builder?"

"Well, I didn't tell them that at first," he said. "I actually did give it a shot and took some classes with that in mind, but being a doctor just wasn't in me so I decided I couldn't fake it any longer."

"And…?" she asked, waiting for him to tell her the rest of the story.

"And eventually, after some raised voices and long arguments, they made their peace with my choice." His mouth curved as he remembered the interaction. "I believe my mother's exact words were that someone had to build the hospitals or doctors would wind up performing patients' surgeries out in the field." His smile grew as he recalled the scene. "My mother liked to exaggerate."

"And your father?" Addie asked. "What did he say about his only child not following in his footsteps?"

"He was never much of a talker," Jason told her. He debated his next words for a moment, then decided that the subject was liable to come up once his cousin returned from his extended honeymoon. "Both of my parents were very proud of Neil. I think they thought of him as the son they never had."

Addie felt her heart constricting for him again.

"I don't think they really thought that way, did they?"

Jason laughed dryly. "You don't know my parents," he told her. But there were no hard feelings. "Lucky thing that Neil and I have always been very close."

Miss Joan picked that moment to swing by the counter to check on them. It was becoming obvious that she regarded Jason as her special project. "So, how's everything?" she asked, her hazel eyes indicating what was left on the plates.

Jason never hesitated. "Just fantastic."

"As always, Miss Joan," Addie said, adding her voice to Jason's declaration.

Miss Joan made a disparaging noise. "You have to say that," she said, looking at Jason. "Otherwise you know that dinner won't be on the house."

That surprised him. He'd been paying for his dinner, as well as Addie's, every time they came to the diner. He had convinced Addie the reason he was paying for it was because they were having a working dinner.

"Dinner's on the house?" Jason asked the woman.

Miss Joan pursed her lips. "Don't play innocent with me, Builder Boy. You knew dinner was on the house when I recommended it. Angel's meals certainly don't need any extra marketing."

"Well, be that as it may, the meal was really great, and please tell Angel we really appreciate her putting two servings aside for us," Jason told the woman.

Miss Joan nodded. "I'll be sure to pass that along when she gets in tomorrow," she said to Jason. And then she lowered her voice as she asked, "I hear that Dr. and Mrs. Eastwood are due back the day after tomorrow. That true?"

Jason feigned amazement. "I thought you knew everything."

"I do," she answered a bit formally. "I was just making polite conversation, not that you'd know anything about that, I guess. You book a room at the hotel yet?"

When Jason looked at her blankly, Miss Joan sighed. "You don't intend to stay at the doctor's house after he comes back with his new bride, do you?" she asked.

The days had been filled with decisions revolving around the new hospital being constructed and taking shape. He hadn't had any time to think about his living situation once Neil and Ellie came back.

"I hadn't thought about it yet," Jason confessed.

"Well, I'd start thinking if I were you, Builder Boy," Miss Joan told him.

An idea suggested itself to Addie. She turned toward him. "You could stay in Ellie's room until the project's completed."

Jason's immediate response was to decline the offer, but Miss Joan interjected, "Sounds like a good idea to me. Ellie takes your place at the good doc's house and you take her place at her grandfather's house." Miss Joan smiled. "Kinda like a game of musical people."

"I can't just invite myself over," Jason protested.

"You didn't," Miss Joan pointed out. "I did." She looked at Addie. "You okay with that?" she asked, even though Addie had been the one to initially bring up the solution. "Because I'm pretty sure your grandfather would be. He owes me."

Addie inclined her head. There was no explanation needed. Miss Joan was referring to her backing off from disciplining Zelda and technically keeping the two apart.

"I'm fine with it," Addie told her.

"Well, Builder Boy, looks like you've got a place to lay your head. And I'll be sure to tell Angel you liked her pork loin," she added as an afterthought as she made her way down the counter toward another customer.

Jason watched Miss Joan walk away for a moment, then looked at Addie. "She really is queen of the castle, isn't she?" he asked. He was smiling as he asked the question.

Addie nodded. "At the very least," she agreed, then decided to give him a verbal tour of his new quarters. "Ellie's bedroom has complete privacy. And you won't have to share a bathroom. I learned how to build things by helping my grandfather add bathrooms to the house," she told him proudly.

There hadn't even been that much of a learning curve, she recalled.

"And he won't mind my living at the house?" Jason asked.

"My grandfather lived with eleven brothers and sisters when he was growing up. He thrived on crowds. He won't even notice that you're there," she promised.

"You know, I can still rent a room at the hotel," Jason said.

"And wind up insulting my grandfather? I wouldn't if I were you," Addie warned him.

"Well, I certainly wouldn't want to insult your grandfather. All right—" Jason nodded "—I accept your hospitality. But I want to be able to run this by your grandfather before I move in, just to make sure."

Addie was completely amenable to that. "My grandfather really appreciates politeness and good manners," she told Jason.

"You know, your grandfather does have that lady friend and he just might mind having a stranger in the house—me, not her," Jason clarified.

She smiled. "I don't think having you there would make him feel self-conscious. Zelda's already been over a couple of times. She's a very quiet person," Addie told Jason, emphasizing her point with a flirtatious wink.

He hadn't thought of the older couple in that light. "Are you saying what I think you're saying?" Jason asked.

She raised her shoulders innocently. "I'm not saying anything. Now shut down that imagination of yours before it winds up getting you in trouble."

He looked at her for a long moment, his expression unreadable, and then said quietly, "I think it already has."

Chapter Sixteen

In deference to Ellie, Jason didn't even consider moving his things into her old room until after she had arrived back from her honeymoon. He wanted his cousin's new wife to be able to move her things into Neil's at a leisurely pace. The last thing he wanted was for Ellie to feel as if she was being rushed or pressured.

If need be, Jason told the newlyweds when they finally all got together at the ranch house, he was more than willing to rent a room at the hotel.

But as it was, that didn't turn out to be the case.

"I'm not about to inconvenience you, Jason,"

Ellie informed him. "In my opinion, you're being a really good sport and very patient about all this, seeing how pressed you are for time."

Jason appeared surprised by her assessment, so Ellie quickly explained.

"Addie told me how hands-on you are…on the job," she added, realizing how her statement might have come across to Neil's cousin. Having been gone for four weeks, Ellie had no real idea just how things were going between her sister and her husband's cousin, but observing the two of them now, she did have her suspicions.

"You know," Eduardo said, catching the tail end of the conversation, "your things can be stored in the barn until they can be transported to the proper rooms." He looked from his granddaughter to Jason. "There is no real hurry to move everything. You can take your time."

Jason was accustomed to living out of a suitcase if the situation called for it, but he doubted that Ellie wanted to go that route.

"I think that as a new wife," Jason began, "Ellie might be eager to settle into her new living quarters as soon as possible so she can set up housekeeping."

"Well, there're four of us," Neil pointed out.

"We can probably get this move done by next Sunday at the latest."

"There are five of us," Eduardo corrected, looking at Neil. "If you are going to be part of the family, you need to get used to the fact that all of us combine our efforts in order to get things accomplished. That is what it means to be a family."

Ellie slipped her arms around her grandfather's waist and gave him a quick, enthusiastic hug.

"Oh, I've missed you, Grandpa," she declared with a warm laugh.

Eduardo returned her affection and patted her arm, then said, "And I have missed you, *querida*. Now, what do you say I make a welcome-home lunch for you two and then we at least begin making plans about moving your things into the proper houses?"

Ellie sat down on the sofa and moved closer to her husband. "Well, you've got me sold. What can I do to help with the meal?" she asked, beginning to get up.

Eduardo indicated that she should take her seat again.

"You can eat it. I did not say that I needed any help," he informed the people in his living room, then went into the kitchen.

"Well, I see that nothing's changed," Ellie told her sister with a smile.

Addie flashed a wider one back. "Oh, I wouldn't say that."

Ellie's brow furrowed. "What's changed?"

Before Addie had a chance to say anything, Jason beat her to it. "You might have noticed the spring in your grandfather's step. He's been keeping company with Zelda…apparently with Miss Joan's blessings."

This latest development managed to take Ellie and her husband completely by surprise. "You're kidding! We've all known that they were sweet on each other, but I didn't think it went any further than that." She lowered her voice as she asked Addie, "Did Grandpa give Miss Joan a dressing-down? Is that why she backed off?"

"No, he didn't have to," Addie told her. "It seems that Harry, Miss Joan's husband, came to the rescue, reminding Miss Joan how people change…including her. He mentioned how she had once sworn that she was never going to get married again, until he finally wore her down and convinced her to take a chance on him."

"Best thing she ever did," Ellie said, putting her two cents in.

"Bless that old man," Ellie declared. "I mean Harry, not Grandpa," she confided.

Neil smiled as he affectionately nuzzled his wife's neck. "Bless all the old men."

Ellie leaned into him. "Amen to that," she murmured.

Jason quietly looked on, observing the couple. For the first time in his life, he found himself envying his cousin, really envying him.

There had been a lot of women in his lifetime. He had never lacked for companionship, but as beautiful as some of the women had been, none of the relationships had ever amounted to anything. He knew without being told that he had never experienced the kind of joy that his cousin was feeling, certainly not anywhere near this intensity.

Without meaning to, Jason glanced at Addie and couldn't help wondering, not for the first time, what it might be like between them. Working with Addie these last few weeks had caused him to experience something he never had before. A very intense spark.

Jason wasn't sure if he was just imagining things because he envied Neil, or if what he was experiencing was actually real.

Well, he had until the end of the project to figure it out, he thought. He just hoped that gave him enough time.

* * *

It was decided that the perfect ending to the celebratory meal that Eduardo had prepared was for Ellie and Neil to begin their new life together at Neil's house.

The decision had come from Jason.

"Just let me swing by the house and get some of my stuff," Jason requested. "And then I'll be out of your hair until such time when it's not inconvenient for me to come by and get the rest of my things."

"I'll go with you," Addie volunteered. "That way you can bring over more. And then we can leave the newlyweds to play house," she said with a grin.

It was still hard for her to get used to the idea that her sister was now officially a married lady, Addie thought. But she was very, very happy for Ellie.

Jason looked at Addie uncertainly. "Are you sure?"

"You should know by now that I wouldn't say it if I didn't mean it," Addie said.

"Sorry," he apologized, doing his best to keep a straight face. "I guess that I'm just a slow learner."

Addie rolled her eyes. "Yeah, right."

Following his cousin and Ellie to Neil's house,

Jason worked quickly, throwing a few items into his suitcase that he would need, such as a change of clothes in the morning.

Addie glanced into his suitcase. There wasn't all that much there. "Are you sure this is all you need?"

"I'm sure," Jason answered.

Picking up his suitcase, he walked out into the hallway. He nodded toward his cousin and Ellie, lowering his voice so that they wouldn't hear him.

"It's obvious that they can hardly keep their hands off each other. That's our cue to go," he urged.

"On behalf of my sister," Addie said once she and Jason were on their way back to the ranch house, "thank you."

Jason shrugged. "It's no big deal. In my case, one bed is as good as another, although obviously, for Ellie and my cousin, it's a whole different matter."

"Can't argue with that," she agreed.

When they drew close to the ranch house, the first thing Addie noticed was that her grandfather's truck was missing.

"Wonder where he went," she said. "I didn't think he would want to miss your first night here."

Getting out of his car, Jason laughed. She made it sound as if Eduardo was his grandfather, as well.

"I'm a big boy," Jason reminded her. "Eduardo probably knows that I can settle in without supervision. Besides," he added with a smile, "I have you."

Addie could have sworn there was a twinkle in his eye.

After walking into the house, Addie turned on the lights and despite the fact that her grandfather's truck was gone, she still scanned the ground floor.

"Grandpa, are you here?" she called out.

"His truck's not here, remember?" Jason pointed out.

"I know, I just thought he might have parked it somewhere that I couldn't see," Addie explained.

And then she saw the note in the center of the table.

Crossing to it, Addie picked up the note and scanned it quickly.

Jason set down his suitcase. "Is it from your grandfather?" he asked.

Addie nodded. Finished, she folded the note and put it into her front pocket.

"What did he say?" Jason asked. "Unless it's something private," he added as the thought occurred to him.

"Well, it's kind of private," she agreed. Before Jason could change the subject, Addie said, "He said he was going over to see Zelda and that I shouldn't wait up for him." She grinned. "The little devil said he might not be in until morning."

"I take it that Zelda doesn't live with Miss Joan and her husband."

Addie laughed. "No, that she does not," she answered. There definitely wouldn't be any "sleepovers" if Zelda did.

This wasn't exactly an ordinary situation for him. "So how do you feel about your grandfather spending the night with a woman?" he asked, curious about her reaction. Thinking back, he doubted if he had ever seen his parents so much as hug, much less kiss.

"Honestly? A little strange, I have to admit. But I'm also happy for him," she added. "That man has been sacrificing his life for Ellie and me for as long as I can remember. It's about time that he focused on enjoying himself." Changing the subject, she said, "Let me show you where your room is."

Jason picked up the suitcase he had just set down. Gesturing ahead, he told Addie, "Lead the way."

"Funny, I was just going to have you wander

around the house until you could guess where the room was located," she joked.

"Very funny," he said. "I can crash on your sofa if you'd prefer."

Addie shook her head. "Can't have that. What if Grandpa decides to bring his lady friend home with him? Can't have your sleeping body be the first thing she sees as she comes through the door. It might throw her."

He wasn't about to ask her to explain that.

"C'mon," Addie urged. "In the interest of modesty, let me show you to your new sleeping quarters."

Addie went up, then glanced to see if Jason was following her.

He was.

The rooms at the top of the stairs went in two different directions. She went to the left and brought Jason over to the second room.

Addie was about to open the door when he suddenly stopped her.

"The room's not decorated all in pink, is it?" Jason asked her.

"And if it was?" she asked.

Addie deliberately put an edge in her voice so he couldn't guess whether or not the room was actu-

ally pink. Doing her best not to laugh, she waited
for Jason to say something.

He made a face. "Well, honestly, it would take
me some getting used to," he confessed. "But I
guess I could live with it."

She finally laughed. "Well, lucky for you, the
room's in Ellie's favorite color—blue," she told
him. "Blue is actually both our favorite color." She
stepped to the side to let him go in first. "Is blue
all right with you?"

"Blue's great with me," Jason acknowledged,
relieved. She had him going for a moment. "I'm
sorry. I didn't want to sound as if I was being un-
grateful."

"You didn't," she said. "I just wanted to see
what you'd say if I yanked your chain. By the way,
just as a point of information, the sheets are fresh.
I changed them the day after Ellie went on her
honeymoon. And there are fresh bathroom tow-
els in the linen closet just down the hall. Anything
else you need?" she asked him.

Belatedly, he set down the suitcase he was still
holding. "Yeah, some company. You feel like staying up and talking for a while?"

Amused, she looked at her watch. It was only
a little after nine. "I think I can manage that, con-

sidering it's not even ten o'clock yet. How early do you think I go to bed?"

"Sorry," he apologized, thinking she might have been insulted. "I normally drop facedown in bed when I get in from work, but seeing as how this is my first day in a new room, it usually takes me at least a day to get used to my new surroundings. Otherwise I can't sleep," he admitted.

She nodded. "Well, that sounds normal enough to me. You up for going downstairs and getting a nightcap?"

"Sure. Just one question," he said.

She assumed that he was going to ask her about what sort of alcohol she had on hand, or something to that effect, which was why his actual question totally threw her.

"Where's your room?" he asked.

Addie smiled mysteriously. "It's in the house."

"Could you be a little more specific than that?" he asked.

"I could," she told him. And then she smiled. "Maybe later."

There was only one reason why she would be so vague. "Don't you trust me?"

She realized that he was being serious. "If I didn't trust you," Addie said as she walked out of the room, "you wouldn't be here. And if my grandfather didn't trust you, you definitely wouldn't be here. Now, is there anything else?"

"Nope," he replied. "You've answered all my questions."

"Good. Now that that's all settled, why don't we go downstairs and get you that drink," Addie proposed.

Jason nodded and followed her. "Sounds good to me."

Chapter Seventeen

"I have to admit that I'm kind of glad that you're here," Addie told Jason.

There was a platter of snacks she had put together on the coffee table and she placed the glass of white wine she had poured for Jason next to it. She knew he wasn't hungry, but the snacks were there to help absorb the alcohol…just in case he asked for a second glass.

What Addie had just said to him really surprised him. Jason was aware of the fact that they were getting along, but this seemed to take their growing friendly relationship to a whole new level.

"Oh?" His curiosity piqued, Jason asked, "Any particular reason you just said that?"

Addie was fairly certain that he would make fun of her for saying what she was about to say, but she was the one who had started it so she had no one to blame but herself.

"To be honest," she began, sitting down beside Jason on the sofa, "I'm not used to coming home to an empty house, at least not in the evening. Either Ellie or my grandfather are usually here. *Were* usually here," she corrected, thinking that was no longer gong to be the case with her sister.

"Sometimes," Addie continued, "they were both here. I guess it's just something I've always taken for granted. Hearing my voice come echoing back to me when I called out to my grandfather when I walked in just didn't feel quite right." Addie shrugged a little too carelessly, then looked away. "You probably think that I'm being infantile."

"No, I don't think that at all," Jason told her, pausing to take a sip of his wine. "We all just get used to different modes of behavior. For instance, when I was a kid, I used to love watching those old-fashioned horror movies—the really hokey ones. And then I wouldn't be able to get to sleep all night. Neil used to lecture me about that, saying the best way not to let those movies keep me up was not to watch those damn things in the first place.

"Since he was the older one…and the wiser one," Jason added with a grin, "eventually I listened to him. I have to admit that I was tempted to watch one of those creepy movies a few times, but I didn't. And then, sure enough, after a while I stopped being afraid.

"Took me a little longer to sleep without having the light on," Jason admitted. "But eventually I did. I was very proud of myself when I conquered that phase." His mouth curved a little as he finished his wine. Setting down the glass, he looked at Addie. "I guess I've just given you something to blackmail me with."

Addie hadn't realized just how nice Jason could actually be. Not to mention how extremely good-looking he was.

"Why would I want to do something like that?" she asked him. "You don't think I'm capable of that sort of behavior, do you?"

He laughed quietly, shaking his head. "I guess I was just thinking of some of the kids I grew up with." Moving aside the empty wineglass, he absently dipped a chip into a container of guacamole and promptly consumed it.

Addie watched as Jason picked up a second chip

and repeated the process. "I didn't realize that you were actually hungry." She had put out the snacks out of habit. Addie glanced toward the refrigerator. "Would you like me to make you a sandwich?" she asked.

Jason hadn't even realized that he had picked up another chip. Finishing it, he dusted off his fingers.

"That's very nice of you, but you really don't have to go to any trouble. I'm not actually hungry," he admitted, even as one last chip disappeared behind his lips.

"Okay," she said, "if you're not hungry, why are you eating?"

He raised his eyes toward hers. For a moment, it didn't seem as if he was going answer her, and then he did. "Nerves, I guess."

"Nerves?" she repeated. She hadn't a clue what he was talking about. She had observed him on the job and he had always been totally cool, calm and in control of the situation, no matter what it was. "What do you have to be nervous about?"

He knew she was referring to their work relationship. Even when they were at the diner, they were usually talking about the job.

"Well, the dynamic is different," Jason began.

Addie still didn't quite understand. "How is it different?"

Jason looked at her pointedly. "Well, this is the first time that we've been alone together."

"We've been alone together before," Addie told him.

"No, not really," he contradicted. "We've been supposedly 'alone,' but it was always a case where people could walk in on us at any time. Besides, we were usually discussing work…*or* working. But this time, it's different. We're not talking about work…or working," Jason pointed out.

She tried to make sense out of what he was telling her. "So, what, you're afraid I'm going to jump you?" she asked him, making no attempt to hide her amusement. "Is that what's making you nervous?"

"No," he answered. Shifting on the sofa, he turned toward Addie. Then, ever so lightly, he combed his fingers through her hair, tilting her face up to his.

And then he kissed her.

"I'm afraid that I might wind up being tempted to do that," he told her. And then Jason stopped himself before he could kiss her again and it led to something else. "Maybe this is a bad idea," he told her, getting up. "Maybe I should just check into that hotel in town." Jason seriously began to get ready to leave.

Addie caught hold of his wrist. "And maybe you should just shut up," she proclaimed. Jason was about to say something in response, but Addie brought her mouth up to his and kissed him with feeling.

This time her heart felt as if it had just slammed hard against her chest.

She wanted to kiss him again.

Jason felt the rush of desire pumping through his veins as, going with instinct, he drew her closer to him. Ever since he had first met her, he had been trying to convince himself that this attraction he was feeling was just something on the surface and that it would fade away in time, the way that all of his attractions eventually did.

But he knew that he was lying to himself, predominantly because underneath it all, he was worried that Addie might not feel the same way about him that he felt about her. To avoid any embarrassment, it was best to pretend that he really wasn't feeling anything at all.

But he did, heaven help him. He did feel something for her. Something very strong and very real. Something unlike anything he had ever felt before.

Tilting her head up, he kissed Addie again, this time with all the passion that he felt surging through him.

The urge increased.

He wanted to do it again—and again—but

with effort, Jason managed to get hold of himself and stop.

Exhaling, he drew back.

He saw confusion and disappointment in Addie's eyes when she looked at him.

The break didn't help. He wanted her even more.

"Are you sure that there's no chance that your grandfather will suddenly come home?" he asked.

"As sure as I could be about anything that my grandfather said. He has always been extremely truthful. To a fault. And we could always go upstairs to your room, or mine," Addie said. "I promise, even if for some reason he does come home, my grandfather has never been known to come bursting into my room or into Ellie's. He has always been very respectful of our space. Certainly respectful of any guest who has stayed here."

She smiled, thinking of the complaints she had heard from some of her friends when they were dating. "That's one of the things that makes my grandfather such a wonderful man."

Jason slowly ran the back of his hand along her cheek. He could feel himself getting aroused all over again. "He definitely gets my vote."

Turning toward the staircase, Jason took her hand in his. But instead of immediately going up, he had one last question. "And this is all right with you?" he asked, his eyes indicating the stairs. He didn't want her to feel as if he was pressuring her.

"You still don't know me, do you?" she asked. "If it wasn't all right with me, right now you'd be lying with your back on the floor and my knee would be pressed against your chest while I told you to never make a move on me again." There was humor in her eyes. "Is any of that happening?"

A smile was beginning to curve his mouth. "No."

"Then I suggest you stop overthinking all this and start going up the stairs before it gets to be daylight. By my estimation, that gives us at least seven hours, if not a little bit more."

His smile grew wider. "Well, I'm convinced."

Addie sighed. "Finally."

Taking his hand back in hers and feeling her heart starting to pound again, Addie led Jason up the stairs.

At the landing, she turned to look at him and asked, "Your room or mine?"

"I want you to feel comfortable," Jason said, "So yours."

Her eyes sparkled "You just want to find out where my room is located."

"Well, there's that, too," he admitted with a smile.

Rather than let her lead him to her room, Jason pulled her into his arms and kissed Addie again. It completely amazed him how much easier that was getting to be with each kiss that was exchanged between them.

"I should have thought about blindfolding you before we came up here," Addie said, deadpan.

"I promise I'll do my best to forget," Jason told her solemnly. Everything but you."

Her eyes were shining. "Nice save," she said as she brought him over to her room. It turned out to be directly on the other side of her sister's room as well as the linen closet.

The moment Addie opened her door, she could feel her heart begin hammering. And when she pushed the door closed again and turned toward Jason, her heart was now pounding double time. Maybe a little more.

Addie was afraid that she wouldn't be able to catch her breath, but somehow, she managed. Weaving her arms around his neck, Addie brought her mouth up to his again.

This time, it felt as if there was literally an explosion going off between them. The kiss grew in intensity until it practically managed to swallow them both up.

Addie didn't remember Jason undressing her,

didn't fully remember pulling his clothes from his body, either.

What she did remember, in glowing terms, was the hunger that reared its head. The hunger that just kept growing and growing with each passing moment that went by, seizing her in its grip.

Within moments, as clothes were discarded and went flying between them, they wound up naked on her bed with their bodies tangled together.

Kissing each other over and over again, their hands stroking one another, they were completely consumed by the passion that continued to grow within them. It grew greater by the moment and showed no signs of slowing down—or vanishing—anytime soon.

Wanting her more than he had ever wanted any other woman in his life, Jason ran his lips along Addie's throat and her chin. And then he slowly worked his way down along her shoulders and the plains along her breasts.

Every slow, methodic pass had her drawing in her breath. Sounds of pleasure emerged as Addie shivered in abject delight.

But as exquisite as all this was, Addie didn't want to just be on the receiving end of it. She wanted to be able to at least reciprocate some of what she was feeling. Seemingly catching Jason off guard, she managed to switch their positions and ran the tip of her tongue along his chest. She felt him shiver in response.

Addie moved down lower and lower, determined to make him feel the waves of delight that he had created within her just moments ago.

She delighted in the way he closed his eyes, delighted in hearing his heavy breathing. It was enough to create large feelings of ecstasy within her.

She allowed her guard to go down, and suddenly, Jason had managed to switch their positions again. Hovering over her, he wound up creating ripples of pure, hot desire. They built up within her until suddenly, she was feeling the first orgasm seize her in its grasp, taking her prisoner.

Addie felt a wave of pure delight sweep over her. It was followed by another, even larger wave.

And another.

Her body trembling, Addie didn't know how much longer she was going to be able to hold out. All she did know was that this was better than anything else she had ever experienced or ever hoped to experience.

Excitement vibrating through her, Addie pulled Jason to her and whispered, "Now. Do it now," hoarsely against his cheek.

Her breath warmed him, creating an incredible

response. His arms tightened around her, reveling in the feel of her hot body against his.

Addie felt rather than saw Jason smile. "With pleasure," he said, answering her plea for him to take her. He slowly drew himself up along her body until his eyes were looking into hers.

Anticipation and excitement, mingled with hunger, pulsated all through him. With careful movements, he parted her legs with his knee, and then very slowly, his eyes still on hers, he entered her.

Once he did, Jason began to move with precision, at first slowly, and then faster and faster.

Addie wrapped her arms around his neck, moving her body right along with his. She could feel the desire building until the uniting explosion finally came, wrapping them both up in a hot, pulsating blanket made up of pure unadulterated ecstasy.

Addie's heart pounded wildly and continued to do so until, ever so slowly, it began to return to a normal beat.

Still, she continued to hold on, reveling in the way the sensation it created echoed through her body.

It was a while before the joy moving through her settled down to a whisper.

Jason continued holding her against him, delighting in the way her heart felt beating against his as it slowly returned to its regular rhythm.

"I wasn't expecting that," he finally whispered against her hair.

Addie raised herself up a little on her elbow to look at him. "Why? Did you think I was going to be a dud?"

"No, of course not," Jason denied. "I just wasn't expecting to feel that level of fulfillment our first time around." He realized that he was tripping over his own tongue and tried again. "I mean, I knew it was going to be good," he amended. "But I had no idea that it was going to be *this* good."

Addie raised her eyebrows. "So I surprised you?"

He laughed softly. "That is putting it mildly," Jason admitted. "You, lady, are the definition of a walking surprise."

Addie's eyes were sparkling as she raised herself up again and looked at him. "Would you happen to be in the mood to do it again?" she asked mischievously.

"Lady, you're going to wind up killing me," he told her. "But, yes," Jason answered as he took her back into his arms. "Again, please."

Chapter Eighteen

Daylight was tiptoeing into the room.

As he opened his eyes, Jason realized that it was nearly dawn. He also realized that Addie was lying next to him, sound asleep. Her arm was stretched across his chest.

Moving very carefully, he lifted her arm from his chest and then tucked it against her side. That done, he let out the breath he was holding. And then, very slowly, he began to slip out of Addie's queen-size bed.

He felt her stirring and froze for a moment, waiting for her to fall back asleep. All he wanted to do was to go into his new room and climb into that bed just in case Addie's grandfather did come home before he had said he would.

Jason believed Addie when she said that her grandfather would never come bursting into her bedroom, but that didn't mean that the man wouldn't come into the room for some unforeseen reason. The last thing he wanted was for the generous old man to find the two of them in bed together. No matter how understanding the man was, Jason just couldn't see that sitting right with Eduardo.

Jason had almost managed to finally get out of bed when he suddenly saw Addie's eyelids open and she was looking at him with those sky-blue eyes of hers.

"Going somewhere?" she asked in a sleepy voice.

"Yes," he answered. "To my new room."

"Was it something I said?" Addie asked, a half smile gracing her lips.

He answered her honestly. "Addie, I don't want to take a chance on your grandfather coming in and finding us in bed together."

"But—" she began to protest, about to repeat what she had already told Jason yesterday.

He was ahead of her. "I know, I know," Jason said, holding up his hand to get her to stop talking. "He's never come bursting into your room before, but I don't want to entertain the possibility that this might wind up being the first time. If nothing else, that would be a terrible way to repay his hospitality."

Addie sat up, tucking the sheet around her chest. She sighed, nodding. "All right, if it makes you feel better about all this, far be it from me to keep you here against your will."

Jason suddenly felt this overwhelming desire to kiss her but held himself in check. He knew exactly where that would wind up leading.

"It's not that I don't want to be 'kept,'" he told her with an endearing, crooked smile. "I just don't think I should possibly ruin what had been, up until now, a very glorious evening."

Tickled, Addie shook her head. "Well, if you put it that way. Go. I'll see you in the morning."

"It is morning," Jason pointed out. That was why he was going to the other bedroom now instead of later.

"Don't quibble over words," Addie said. "Just go before I'm tempted to drag that sexy body of yours back into my bed so you can have your way with me again."

Jason felt fresh ripples of desire undulating through his system, unsettling his stomach. But he forced himself to leave, knowing that if he lingered even a moment longer, he definitely wouldn't be able to go.

So, fighting the urge to press one last deep kiss to her lips, Jason walked out of Addie's bedroom.

"So how was your first night in your new bed?" Eduardo asked Jason later that morning.

Jason and Addie had deliberately come down a few minutes apart. Addie's grandfather was already in the kitchen. He had put on the coffee and was in the middle of preparing breakfast for the three of them.

The question had caught him off guard, and Jason was unclear how to respond to the man. Did Eduardo actually know what had transpired last night, or was he just asking a random, innocent question?

At a loss, Jason took his cue from Addie. She had just poured three cups of coffee, one for each of them, then brought the cups over to the kitchen table. She placed a steaming cup at each of their seats.

"I heard Jason tossing and turning for a while last night," she told her grandfather. "You know how it is when you're sleeping in a new bed for the first time."

"I certainly do," the older man acknowledged. He was scrambling three eggs along with chopped-up bits of ham, a sprinkling of cheddar cheese and several slices of bacon in a giant skillet. Glancing over his shoulder, he told Jason, "You'll get used to it."

"I'm sure I will," Jason answered. He still had no idea if Addie's grandfather was just voicing empty platitudes, or if the man had actually guessed that he and Addie had spent at least part of the night together. He decided that it was safer for all of them if he just played innocent.

By the time Monday morning rolled around, the tension Jason had been experiencing had lessened considerably. He had finally begun to relax a little, taking a philosophical view of the situation.

It also helped that he was able to return to what had become familiar surroundings for him.

Progressing on a project had always been a panacea for him. This time, both Jason and Addie were able to throw themselves into the ongoing project, making even more headway on it than either one of them had thought was possible, especially Addie.

There was less carpentry for her to do because Jason wanted her more focused on finding MRI machines and similar apparatus for the new hospital. Thanks to her success with the company run by Albert Hobbs, word of mouth had spread and Addie found that she was able to line up more X-ray machines at reasonable prices. That allowed the new hospital to purchase more items than had initially been expected.

On his end, Jason found that the people he had hired to work on the hospital had not lost any of their enthusiasm. If anything, their enthusiasm had increased. Everyone, to a person, all seemed to be eager to get the new hospital up and running, ready to be filled at maximum capacity if need be.

As for himself, Jason silently acknowledged that he was eager for that to happen, as well. But, at the same time, he found the idea of that taking place just a little bit daunting. That would mean, quite plainly, that the project was on its way to being completed.

This would mark the very first time that he wasn't a hundred percent focused on finishing a project and moving on.

The idea of moving on, of leaving this crew of people, including his cousin and his wife, Eduardo and, most of all, Addie, filled him with almost a sense of sadness that was an entirely new sensation for him.

He wasn't used to that feeling.

Every single other time, the idea of completing a project and beginning a new one had always filled him with satisfaction and an anticipation that all but lit him up from the inside out.

However, that wasn't the case this time. If anything, Jason toyed with the idea of slowing down.

That was *entirely* against his usual way of operating.

Working with him and checking in on a regular basis, Addie had detected that something was off with Jason. She decided not to probe him. But after a week had gone by, she thought that while she had been more than understanding, she needed some answers…even if it turned out that she didn't like those answers.

Walking by the small area that Jason had claimed as his office, she stuck her head in, recalling the first time she had done that. Had it only been just a little over a couple of months ago? It felt as if an eternity had passed.

"Anything I can do?" she asked him point-blank.

Preoccupied, Jason hardly looked up. "You get an answer about that laboratory equipment yet?" he asked.

That wasn't what was on his mind, but he decided it would do for now. He didn't want to talk about what was actually on his mind.

She decided to answer his question first. "I did," she told him.

Jason raised his eyebrows. "And?"

"And the answer is yes," she told him, then added, "Because we're buying the equipment in bulk, Mr. Hobbs's company can sell it to us at cost."

Jason was genuinely pleased to hear the information. He tried to appear enthusiastic. "That's great news."

She studied him for a long moment. "You don't look as if you think it's great. Seriously, what's wrong?"

He was about to tell her that nothing was wrong, but then the words just wouldn't emerge. "Honestly?" he asked, lowering his voice so that the workers within earshot wouldn't be able to hear.

"No, lie to me," Addie quipped. "Yes, of course honestly." Jason took hold of her arm and led her to an unpopulated corner as she continued talking.

"In case you haven't noticed, boss man, I care about what's going on with you, or is that something I'm not supposed to admit?" she asked. "Because I know that some guys get spooked by admissions like that."

He was glad he'd thought to take this conversation elsewhere. Her honesty had caught him off guard. So much so that he asked, "Didn't anyone teach you how to play games?"

She thought that was rather an odd thing to ask. Something was off, she decided. "Sure. Solitaire, poker and a whole bunch of kid games."

Jason frowned, exasperated. "I'm not talking about those kind of games."

"I know," she answered solemnly. "And I don't believe in the kind of games you're referring to. I was taught that the key to everything was always honesty. In case I didn't mention it, I happen to be a great believer in honesty. Now, once more with feeling. What's on your mind?"

Jason sighed. "I can see the end of the tunnel."

"Ok-a-a-ay," Addie responded, drawing the word out and waiting for him to jump in and clarify what he was talking about. "I still don't understand what the exact problem is."

He looked off into space rather than at her. "Every time I came close to wrapping things up, close to the end," he emphasized, "that always used to fill me with a great feeling of accomplishment."

There was no light in his eyes, she thought. "So what's the problem this time?" she asked, knowing that every aspect of the project was not just going according to schedule, it was actually going *ahead* of schedule.

"The problem is that feeling of accomplishment, of elation and triumph, it seems to be gone. I'm just not feeling it. Instead, I'm actually experiencing a feeling of dread, of loss, if you will." He looked at her to see if he was making himself clear. "This is really out of character for me."

"Maybe the answer is very simple," she told him.

"Okay, enlighten me."

"It's because you don't want this job to end. You don't want to move on," Addie explained.

She had managed to hit the nail on the head, Jason thought grudgingly, but he didn't want to admit it. Not to himself and certainly not to her. She'd undoubtedly think that there was something wrong with him, especially since when they had started, he had extolled what a great feeling it was to be on the cusp of completing a project. Moreover, he'd gone on endlessly about how great it felt to be anticipating the next project that was coming down the road.

Instead, he found himself dreading the completion, dreading moving on.

What the hell was going on with him? Jason silently demanded.

"But I always like anticipating the next job down the line," he argued. "I always *liked* moving on."

"Maybe all those other times you viewed staying in one place as stagnating. You wanted to experience that surging feeling of moving on to something new.

"But this time," Addie mused, "it's different for you. Maybe this time you aren't looking forward to moving on," she suggested.

Jason didn't seem convinced.

"People do change, you know," she said.

He pulled back his shoulders. This was much too close to the truth for comfort and he didn't like it. It went totally against his self-image. "I don't," he protested.

"The last time I looked, you were a person," she said, referring to her previous statement. Addie smiled at him. "I'm pretty sure about that." And then she softened. "I know it's scary."

Jason shook his head. "You're wrong," he told her.

Her first reaction was to tell him that she wasn't, that he was just fighting her too hard on this. But she knew that route would only lead to an argument on his part.

Or maybe even worse.

So what she said in response, as she raised her shoulders in a shrug, was "It's been known to happen. And, if it helps you any, you *are* on the way to wrapping up this very important project, which means that you're free to line up another project and move on. If that's what you really want," she added. Her eyes held his for just a moment.

"Now, I need to call a supplier about getting the hospital a whole bunch of tongue depressors and syringes," she told Jason as she left his room.

He watched her go.

Damn it, he had wanted to kiss her before she left, but the opportunity hadn't really presented itself. Just like the opportunity to make love to her at night had managed to elude him for the last couple of days.

Jason felt as if his brain was all scrambled. He needed to get his priorities straight and untangled, he lectured himself.

What he really needed, he thought, was Addie.

The next moment he told himself that maybe he was just building all this up in his head and making far too much of it. His making love with Addie might have just colored everything.

Maybe he was putting far more significance to the lovemaking than was actually there, he thought. Maybe all that was needed to make everything clear and put into proper prospective was just one more night together.

And he had just the place for it, Jason decided with a smile. He was going to book a room at the hotel for them so that there were no worries about her grandfather needing to come in for some unknown reason, and no undue tension.

It would just be the two of them, he reasoned. Clothing would be optional.

His smile grew as he reached for his cell phone. He wasn't even going to tell Addie about this until he had everything in place. It would take some doing on his part, but he should have the reservation for the end of the week.

His smile grew wider as his fingers flew over the cell phone keys.

Chapter Nineteen

As she settled into Jason's car for what she assumed was the ride home at the end of the day, Addie realized that he wasn't going to the ranch house.

"Just where are we going?" she asked him, curious.

Another week had gone by. Another week that brought them closer to the end—of the project and, just as likely, of their relationship, although, lately, he hadn't mentioned anything about either.

She had no idea what that meant.

Addie found herself wavering between hope and resignation. Hope that maybe, just maybe, Jason had made the decision to stay on in Forever, at least for a while. That didn't automatically mean that he would no longer keep on working on a variety of building projects. She was perfectly fine with having him go wherever the work was. But once each project was completed, she was hoping that he would return to his "new" home.

The resignation she was experiencing came in when she concluded that once the hospital was up and running and the celebration over that accomplishment had taken place, Jason would be moving on to the next project.

Forever—and she—would be in his rearview mirror.

It was nothing against her, Addie told herself. It was just the way that Jason was. In his own fashion, Jason was like the mountain climber who was always looking toward the next mountain he wanted to scale and conquer.

Even though, intellectually, she could understand that desire, she just couldn't help wishing that being with her could somehow replace that urge of his to keep moving.

Glancing in Addie's direction, Jason smiled at her question. "I thought that maybe we could treat ourselves to a weekend at the hotel," he told her.

Addie stared at him. Was he kidding? "Pull over," she said to Jason.

That was not the response he was expecting. Maybe he had just caught her off guard, he thought. "What?"

"Pull over," Addie repeated, her voice a little more emphatic.

Jason did as she asked, pulling over to the edge of the road. "Okay, I've pulled over," he said, turning off the engine. "Now would you mind telling me why?"

Addie tried to put this as delicately as she could.

"Don't get me wrong. Going to a hotel for the weekend is a really sweet idea," she began gently.

"Then why—?"

Addie interrupted him. "Let me finish," she said. "It's obvious that you don't come from a small town."

"You already know that," he reminded her, trying to pin her down to answer his question. He still didn't see what was wrong.

"People in small towns thrive on gossip." She didn't like it, but she understood it and she didn't want to feed the gossip mill. "If you and I are seen going to a hotel together, the only hotel in town," she reminded him, "there will be no end to the speculation and gossip around that. It might even continue until one of us—probably me—is dead."

"I didn't think that a little gossip would bother you," he protested. She had struck him as being more independent than that.

"It wouldn't if there was no one else to consider. But I'm not alone in this," Addie explained. "I need to think how something like this would affect my grandfather and Ellie, especially now."

She had lost him, Jason thought. "What makes 'now' so different?"

She looked at him in surprise. Was she the only one who knew? "Neil didn't tell you?"

Jason shook his head impatiently. "Obviously not. Tell me what?"

"Well, they did just find out today," Addie mused. She saw his impatience increasing, so she got straight to it. "You're going to be a second uncle, or grand-uncle or whatever it is that the father's cousin is called these days."

Jason's mouth dropped open. He appeared totally stunned as the news began to penetrate. "They're having a baby?" he cried.

He saw Addie's smile grow as wide as he had ever seen it. Her eyes sparkled as she echoed, "They're having a baby."

"When?" he asked, barely aware of saying the word.

"By Neil's calculation, eight months from now,"

she told him. "Which means that I have seven months to learn how to fly Ellie's plane so I can take over and keep her business going."

He definitely had not seen this coming. At least not so quickly. "I didn't know you could fly."

"I can't—hence the 'learn' part. But what that also means is that I can't be seen going into hotel rooms with impossibly sexy men, or going off to work on out-of-town projects with them, either. At least not in the foreseeable future," Addie told him sadly.

Jason looked at her for a long moment, digesting this completely unexpected news. "Is there anything in that can't-be-seen list that says anything about not being able to have that so-called sexy man come sneaking into your bedroom at night?" he asked, looking into her eyes.

"I thought you didn't want to risk having my grandfather come 'bursting' into my room," she reminded him, struggling to keep a straight face.

"Desperate times require desperate measures," Jason said philosophically. "Besides, after living in your grandfather's house for the last six weeks, I've managed to become convinced that the man is not about to 'burst' into either one of our rooms. At least he hasn't so far."

Well, Addie thought, trying to comfort herself,

Jason might still be leaving after the project finally came to an end, but at least they could be together until he did and at least that was something.

She smiled at him. "Does this mean that I can be expecting a gentleman caller dropping by tonight?"

Jason turned his key in the ignition and restarted his vehicle. "You can definitely count on it," he told her.

When Jason pulled up at the ranch house a little while later, Addie's grandfather's truck was nowhere to be seen. She felt rather disappointed. She had been looking forward to sharing Ellie's news with the man.

"Looks like our good news is going to have to wait a while longer," she told Jason as he turned off his vehicle and she got out.

"You know what else that means, don't you?" Jason asked with a grin.

He began to lock up his car, then stopped. He really needed to remember to be more trusting while he was in Forever.

For the most part, he had managed to do that, but every now and then, he forgot. He knew that Addie noticed.

"No, tell me," Addie told him, feigning innocence.

"I think that I'd rather show you," Jason replied.

She turned her face up to his just before they went into the house, then drew away before their lips could touch.

"Please do," she murmured, then deliberately sexily sauntered off in front of him and into the house.

Addie was determined to make the most of every moment they still had together. She wasn't about to delude herself and pretend that this was going to last forever. Most men didn't think the same way that women did, believing that what they did was only asking for heartache, Addie thought.

But the project still had at least another couple of weeks left, and until that had gone by, she was going to pretend that Jason wouldn't leave right after the new hospital officially opened its doors, something that everyone, including her up until now, had eagerly been anticipating.

Walking into the ranch house, despite the fact that her grandfather's truck was missing, Addie still called out to him. Mentally, she crossed her fingers that he wasn't going to respond.

Much as she wanted to share the good news

about Ellie and Neil with him, she felt that it could keep for a few more hours. She needed to be with Jason, to carve out a few more hours of lovemaking to sustain her so that when he did finally leave, she would have that much more to hold on to.

She had never honestly felt that way about any of the men who had come into her life. For one reason or another, the good times eventually faded and she would move on. Sometimes it was by mutual consent, sometimes it was her own decision, although she was always kind when she broke it off.

The point was that she had never loved any of them nearly as much as she loved Jason. That had turned out to be a real surprise for her.

She tried to comfort herself with the fact that some people went their whole lives not even remotely feeling what she was feeling now.

Thinking that, Addie felt a lump forming in her throat.

"Something wrong?" Jason asked her, noting how unnaturally quiet she had become.

Addie took a breath. "Yes. You're wasting time," she told him, then added, "You're not moving fast enough."

His eyes crinkled as he grinned at her. "Okay, race you up the stairs."

She pretended to nod her approval. "That's better," Addie said just as she picked up the pace, managing to sprint ahead of him.

Jason quickly caught up, reaching the top of the stairs a hair's breadth ahead of her.

Still, the way she had taken the stairs struck him as remarkable.

"Where do you get all this energy?" he asked.

Mischief danced in her eyes as Addie answered him with a single word. "Anticipation."

Jason caught her up in his arms and carried her into her room. "I guess there's a lot of that going around," he told her, setting her down next to her bed.

He began to undress her.

Addie lost no time in returning the favor. She pulled off his clothes so quickly, she came very close to ripping three of the buttons off his shirt.

His hands covered hers, momentarily holding them in place.

"Hey, slow down," Jason told her with a laugh. "Your grandfather's with Zelda, and that means we've got all night."

She knew that, but she also knew that their number of nights together was limited.

"Waste not, want not," Addie told him just before she urgently pressed her mouth against his.

It was as if a gun had gone off, signaling the beginning of their night together. Jason saw no point in holding back any longer. He had been anticipating this from the moment he had planned their getaway to the hotel.

Needs and desires were exploding within his veins, demanding that he claim what he felt in his heart was already his.

They made love like two people who had been celibate all too long instead of two people who knew exactly what was ahead of them.

But they turned out to be wrong.

Their lovemaking practically took on a life of its own. It continued to grow and build in strength until it reached a point where it all but consumed them.

And still it grew.

They had no sooner come to the gratifying pinnacle of their lovemaking than, after a few moments, without a single word passing between them, just a consenting look in their eyes, their torrid, gratifying dance began all over again from the beginning.

This time, when their all-consuming lovemaking finally came to its delicious end, the sound of satisfied, heavy breathing echoed in the air all around them.

Content beyond words, Jason slipped his arm around her shoulders, gently drawing her closer to him.

Addie heard him chuckle quietly to himself as he brushed a kiss to her hair. "Just when I think that you and I have hit a really gratifying high point, that it can't possibly get any better between us," he said, pausing to give her another kiss, "it does. Talk about being surprised."

Her eyes smiled at him as she sighed, forcing herself to focus exclusively on the immediate moment and nothing else.

Focusing on anything more than that would just remind her that all of this had a finite point. What was between them would end all too soon and if she thought about that, she was certain that she wouldn't be able to hold back the tears. The situation would prove far too depressing for her to think about.

"I guess we're just lucky that way," Addie said, snuggling against him.

Jason raised her chin so that he could look into her eyes.

"Yes," he answered, "I guess we are. That's something to think about."

"Jason," Addie said, running the tip of her finger along the outline of his lips.

"Yes?"

"Less talking, more doing," she told him, turning her body into his.

She was about to kiss him when he caught her by her shoulders, holding her back just a little.

"You could actually do this again?" he asked in what could only be construed as disbelief.

Her smile filtered into her eyes. She was determined not to allow Jason to see how sad the idea of his leaving made her.

"Why don't we just give it a try and see?" Addie proposed.

He was about to respond, but she put an end to anything he was about to say by kissing him with a fervor that all but curled his toes.

Any doubts he might have had that she was capable of going another round with him were quickly laid to rest. He wasn't a hundred percent sure about himself, but Jason had no doubts about the woman in his arms.

Digging deep into himself, Jason found a hunger that propelled him to go yet one more final round with Addie.

He made love to her, and with her, as if there was no tomorrow because, for all he knew, by the time they came to the end of this, there just might not be.

What amazed Jason, just before he stopped thinking altogether, was just how much he still wanted Addie, even if this *was* their fourth time around.

Chapter Twenty

There were none of the usual signs indicating that her grandfather was home when Addie got up the following morning. She hurried through her shower and got dressed, thinking it was rather odd that she didn't smell any breakfast being prepared.

Not only that, but the coffee maker was also eerily dormant.

Addie stood in the center of the kitchen, her hands fisted at her waist as she looked around. Concerned, she bit her lower lip. Her grandfather was a notoriously early riser.

"Okay, Grandpa, should I be getting worried?" she murmured to herself.

"Who are you talking to?" Jason asked as he walked in right behind her.

"Nobody, apparently," Addie answered, turning to glance at Jason. "It looks like Grandpa didn't come home last night."

"He does leave notes for you, remember?" Jason pointed out. "And he's done that several times now."

"I know, but he's always turned up the next morning. Early. He's not a young man, Jason. What if something's happened to him?" she asked, several possibilities already crowding into her head.

Jason raised an eyebrow. "You're making noises like a parent," he told her.

"No, I'm making noises like a worried granddaughter," she corrected him pointedly. "He's dedicated to working with his horses. My grandfather never misses a day of work. He made sure that he instilled that same work ethic in us when we were growing up."

As far as Jason saw, there was a simple solution to that. "Why don't you call his cell phone?" he suggested.

Frowning to herself, Addie sighed. "I can't," she told Jason,

"Look, you're worried about him. I'm sure your grandfather will understand this minor invasion of his privacy."

Addie shook her head—Jason had misunderstood the problem. "No, I can't call his cell phone because he doesn't *have* a cell phone."

"That does complicate matters somewhat," he agreed. "I'm assuming that your grandfather's staying at Zelda's. Do you have Zelda's number? Or maybe you could call Miss Joan. She always seems to be on top of everything," Jason said.

Addie nodded, reaching for her cell phone. She'd call Zelda. She was about to tell Jason that was a very good suggestion when she heard the front door opening.

Addie swung around, expecting to see her grandfather walking in. She was about to ask the man why he hadn't called her to say he was going to be late.

The words froze on her tongue.

Her grandfather wasn't alone.

An almost shy-looking Zelda was walking right beside him.

Caught off guard, Addie congratulated herself on recovering quickly.

"Zelda, I didn't realize that Grandpa would be bringing you here this morning. I was just about to make breakfast," she said as she opened the refrigerator. "What would you like?"

"I'll make coffee," Jason volunteered, moving to take the container of coffee out of the refrigerator.

Addie raised her eyebrows. "And the surprises never stop coming."

"That's all right, Addie," Zelda told her, stopping her. "Your grandfather and I have already had breakfast." A conspiratorial smile flashed between the older couple. "I didn't think he should make an announcement on an empty stomach."

"Announcement?" Addie repeated uncertainly. She could only think of one reason for Zelda to say what she had just said. "Then you know?" Addie hadn't realized that her sister must have already gotten in contact with their grandfather, but it did make sense.

Eduardo looked at her, slightly confused by Addie's choice of words. "Of course, I know. After all, I'm the one who proposed."

"Hold it," Addie cried, putting up her hand to stop him from continuing on this path. "Back up," she told her grandfather. "You proposed? To Zelda?"

"Yes, of course," Eduardo told his granddaughter, puzzled by her question. "What did you think I was talking about?"

"The *other* surprise," Jason told Addie's grandfather, trying to untangle the obvious confusion.

Eduardo looked from his granddaughter to Jason, a huge smile taking over every square inch of his features. His eyes were gleaming. "You mean that you and Addie…?"

"No, no," Addie said quickly before her grandfather could finish his question. She didn't need her grandfather making assumptions about them that didn't have a prayer of happening. "We're talking about Ellie and Neil's surprise."

Eduardo looked confused all over again. "All right, you have lost me. I think I will have that coffee now."

Equally confused, Zelda glanced at her new fiancé quizzically. "Is your family always like this?"

Eduardo laughed, amused. "This is one of Addie's good days," he explained to Zelda. "Thank you for explaining things," he said to Jason. "Now, what is this good news about Ellie?"

"She's going to have a baby," Addie announced before Jason could say anything.

"This is wonderful," Eduardo cried, overjoyed at the prospect of his first great-grandchild. "We have to go see her," he told Zelda, his mind racing to assimilate what he viewed to be fantastic news.

Addie nodded, deliberately avoiding Jason's

gaze. "The four of you can exchange your good news," she told her grandfather. With that, she hugged him hard. "I'm really happy for you, Grandpa." Once she released him, she turned toward Zelda. "And for you, Zelda," she said, hugging the woman, as well.

Once they stepped back, Addie eyed her grandfather and cautiously asked, "Does Miss Joan know?"

Eduardo nodded. "I thought it only right to ask her for her blessing." He smiled at the couple in front of him. "To my surprise, she gave it."

Jason could only shake his head in wonder. "I guess that really qualifies as a miracle."

Addie definitely couldn't argue with that, she thought, infinitely relieved that Miss Joan had done an about-face.

"That it is." Changing topics, she told Jason, "Now we have even more of a reason to finish up the hospital—so Ellie doesn't have all that far to go when it's time for her to deliver her baby."

Jason laughed. He thought of the way that Addie had characterized his work ethic. "Now who's being obsessively dedicated?"

Addie feigned ignorance. "I have no idea what you're talking about." She turned toward her grandfather and his fiancée—it felt really strange thinking of them in those terms, but she was thrilled that her grandfather had finally found someone to share his life with.

"When we get back from working on the hospital, we are all going to have a proper celebration for you and Zelda...and for Ellie and Neil." Addie smiled at the older couple. "This is almost too much happiness to deal with all at once," she explained, then kissed her grandfather and Zelda again. "See you both tonight," she told the couple with a broad wink.

The moment they left the ranch house and were in his car, Jason regarded Addie. She had said all the right things back there, but he still felt that something was rather off.

"I think it's really great that your grandfather found someone," Jason said. "He's been alone much too long."

Addie bristled just a little. "He wasn't exactly alone. He had Ellie and me."

"I didn't mean to insult you and your sister," he told her quickly. "But you have to admit it's not the same thing as having a partner to go through life with."

Jason made it sound as if he was an expert when it came to having a significant other in his life. Before she could stop herself, she asked, "And what would you know about that?"

"I know I've never had one," Jason admitted.

For a second, Addie relented and she felt sorry for him. But then she reminded herself that he had never had a significant other in his life by choice.

She gave him a way out that required no commitment.

"Maybe you can live vicariously through Neil and Ellie," she suggested.

"Maybe," he agreed, but there was no enthusiasm in his voice. "Or maybe I want something else."

Was he toying with her, or just giving voice to his confused feelings?

Addie felt as if she was being tortured.

But if she came out and told him how she felt about him, and he didn't feel the same way, she knew she would never be able to survive the hurt. All attempts at working together these final few weeks or so would immediately crash and burn. Despite the happiness she was feeling for her grandfather and her sister, she *knew* she would be completely miserable...and alone.

Addie knew she wouldn't be able to put up with it.

"Well, when you figure it out," she told him in her best civil, removed voice, "be sure to let me know."

* * *

"It looks like this hospital is going to be completed even ahead of my revised projected schedule," Jason told Addie with pride.

They had finally called it a day, locking up the almost completed new hospital. After stopping to pick up the cake Addie had ordered bright and early this morning, they were finally on their way back to the ranch house, and the celebration.

Addie felt her stomach tightening before she could stop it.

"Have you picked out your next project yet?" she asked him, trying not to sound agitated. Mentally, she crossed her fingers that he hadn't, but she knew him better than that.

"In a manner of speaking," Jason answered.

"Is it out of state?" she asked. It was the first thing that came to mind and Addie braced herself for the answer.

Jason spared her a glance, his expression totally unreadable. "Not sure yet."

He was being deliberately vague, she thought. She decided to switch gears and put him on notice. "Because as much as I would like to help you work on the next project," she told him, "you know I can't." Addie repeated what she had already told him once before—if not twice. "Things have changed. Ellie's going to need me—to help her with her business *and* to help with the baby."

Jason nodded. "I know that."

Damn, she could feel her stomach muscles tightening. But she pushed on. "How soon before you leave?" she asked him, really trying to brace herself.

He kept his eyes on the road. "I'm not sure. It all depends."

Her frustration began building. "Don't you have any answers?"

Jason shrugged. "Not until I get one of my own, I guess."

Now he was just resorting to word games. "And what answer is that?" she asked. Before he said anything, she spelled it out for him. "What answer do you need to hear?"

Jason had never been a coward before. After all, he had gone up against his parents. They had had great expectations of him, and he had dashed those by telling them that he was dropping out of medical school. At the time he had been fully aware that he was going against all their hopes for him. But continuing in medical school would have made him feel as if he was about to dive off a cliff and right onto the rocks below.

Rebuilding things, not people, was his calling.

Glancing at Addie, he suddenly pulled over to the side of the road.

It was now or never.

"The word *yes*," he told her.

Addie stared at him. He wasn't making any sense, she thought. "What?"

Each word took effort, but he needed to say them. "I want to hear the word *yes* from you," Jason told her.

Addie blew out a breath. She would need this spelled out for her because she was afraid that she was about to answer the wrong question. She refused to allow her own hopes to lead her down the wrong path.

"Yes to what?" she asked him, never taking her eyes off his face.

Jason looked at her, resigned. "You're really going to make this hard for me, aren't you?"

"I don't know, am I?" Addie asked.

Jason blew out a breath. It didn't help his state of mind any, but he pushed on. "Adelyn Montenegro, will you marry me?"

Addie continued staring at him, the silence all but engulfing him.

It continued, and Jason had never felt as if he was on shakier ground.

"Say something," he finally urged.

Addie's eyes met his. "You have to ask?"

He had no idea what that meant. Just as he was about to make some sort of a response, Addie fired another question at him.

"Do you think I just hop into bed with anyone?" she demanded.

He hadn't meant to imply that. "I—"

"Well, I don't," she informed him. "I've been in a number of relationships, but they only went so far and no further," she said. "And definitely not like what happened between us—the highs, the lows and the lovemaking, all that was a completely different experience with you."

Jason was trying to piece things together and make some sort of sense out of them so that he had the answer he realized that he desperately wanted and needed.

"Then it's yes?" he asked, hardly able to believe that this was actually going his way.

Addie rolled her eyes. "Yes, you big dumb jerk, it's always been yes."

"Then why didn't you say anything?" he asked, stunned.

"What, you were waiting for me to drop to one knee and propose? This is a brand-new world we're living in," she told him, "but some things just remain the way they've always been. Besides, if I asked that all-important question and you turned me down, there went our friendship, up in flames."

Sliding closer in his truck, Jason pulled her into his arms. "You've just described what I've been going through in my head. It's all been very scary," he told Addie, kissing her with feeling.

And then he pulled back after a moment. "Looks like it's been an eventful twenty-four hours," he told her. Suddenly recalling what they had picked up for the celebration, he turned on the engine and said, "We'd better get the cake to the ranch house before it starts dissolving."

"It'll keep for a few more minutes," she told him, an invitation clearly echoing in her voice.

Jason turned off the engine again. "The lady is right again…as usual," he said just before he drew her back into his arms and covered her lips with his own.

It was a while before the builder turned the ignition back on. He was far too busy focusing on building what really counted: their future together.

* * * * *

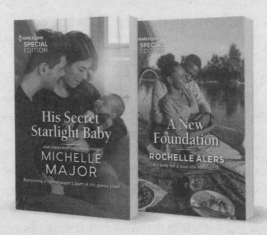

#2875 DREAMING OF A CHRISTMAS COWBOY
Montana Mavericks: The Real Cowboys of Bronco Heights
by Brenda Harlen

In the Christmas play she wrote and will soon star in, Susanna Henry gets the guy. In real life, however, all-grown-up Susanna is no closer to hooking up with rancher Dean Abernathy than she was at seventeen. Until a sudden snowstorm strands them together overnight in a deserted theater...

#2876 SLEIGH RIDE WITH THE RANCHER
Men of the West • by Stella Bagwell

Sophia Vandale can't deny her attraction to rancher Colt Crawford, but when it comes to men, trusting her own judgment has only led to heartbreak. Maybe with a little Christmas magic she'll learn to trust her heart instead?

#2877 MERRY CHRISTMAS, BABY
Lovestruck, Vermont • by Teri Wilson

Every day is Christmas for holiday movie producer Candy Cane. But when she becomes guardian of her infant cousin, she's determined to rediscover the real thing. When she ends up snowed in with the local grinch, however, it might take a Christmas miracle to make the season merry...

#2878 THEIR TEXAS CHRISTMAS GIFT
Lockharts Lost & Found • by Cathy Gillen Thacker

Widow Faith Lockhart Hewitt is getting the ultimate Christmas gift in adopting an infant boy. But when the baby's father, navy SEAL lieutenant Zach Callahan, shows up, a marriage of convenience gives Faith a son and a husband! But she's already lost one husband and her second is about to be deployed. Can raising their son show them love is the only thing that matters?

#2879 CHRISTMAS AT THE CHÂTEAU
Bainbridge House • by Rochelle Alers

Viola Williamson's lifelong dream to run her own kitchen becomes a reality when she accepts the responsibility of executive chef at her family's hotel and wedding venue. What she doesn't anticipate is her attraction to the reclusive caretaker whose lineage is inexorably linked with the property known as Bainbridge House.

#2880 MOONLIGHT, MENORAHS AND MISTLETOE
Holiday, Oregon • by Wendy Warren

As a new landlord, Dr. Gideon Bowen is more irritating than ingratiating. Eden Berman should probably consider moving. But in the spirit of the holidays, Eden offers her friendship instead. As their relationship ignites, it's clear that Gideon is more mensch than menace. With each night of Hanukkah burning brighter, can Eden light his way to love?

YOU CAN FIND MORE INFORMATION ON UPCOMING HARLEQUIN TITLES, FREE EXCERPTS AND MORE AT HARLEQUIN.COM.

HSECNM1121

"You're cold," Dean realized, when Susanna drew her
knees up to her chest and wrapped her arms around her
legs, no doubt trying to conserve her own body heat as
she huddled under the blanket draped over her shoulders
like a cape.

"A little," she admitted.

"Come here," he said, patting the space on the floor
beside him.

She hesitated for about half a second before scooting
over, obviously accepting that sharing body heat was the
logical thing to do.

But as she snuggled against him, her head against
his shoulder, her curvy body aligned with his, there was
suddenly more heat coursing through his veins than Dean

had anticipated. And maybe it was the normal reaction for a man in close proximity to an attractive woman, but this was *Susanna*.

He wasn't supposed to be thinking of Susanna as an attractive woman—or a woman at all.

She was a friend.

Almost like a sister.

But she's not your sister, a voice in the back of his head reminded him. *So there's absolutely no reason you can't kiss her.*

Don't do it, the rational side of his brain pleaded. *Kissing Susanna will change everything.*

Change is good. Necessary, even.

When Susanna tipped her head back to look at him, obviously waiting for a response to something she'd said, all he could think about was the fact that her lips were *right there*. That barely a few scant inches separated his mouth from hers.

He only needed to dip his head and he could taste those sweetly curved lips that had tempted him for so long, despite all of his best efforts to pretend it wasn't true.

Not that he had any intention of breaching that distance.

Of course not.

Because this was *Susanna*.

No way would he ever—

Apparently the signals from his brain didn't make it to his mouth, because it was already brushing over hers.

Don't miss
Dreaming of a Christmas Cowboy *by Brenda Harlen,
available December 2021 wherever
Harlequin Special Edition books and ebooks are sold.*

Harlequin.com